THE *Wedding* GUEST

R.W. HART

To order additional copies of this book, contact:
Bookwhip
1-855-339-3589
https://www.bookwhip.com

ONE WEEK EARLIER

$\mathcal{A}$manda Pike stood in front of the full length mirror in her bedroom trying on a variety of clothes while deciding what to pack for her upcoming trip. The disappointment she felt because her outfits seemed to have shrunk while hanging in the closet did little to temper her excitement. She saved the most important article of clothing needed for the trip to try on last. Her reflection in the mirror was not the look she had hoped for. After a few moments she took a deep breath and then gave a dejected sigh as she muttered. "I definitely need a new swimsuit." Amanda tried to adjust the swimsuit to bring the *girls* to the height they were the last time she had gone swimming. She turned to the left and then to the right as she adjusted the swimsuit bottom and checked the reflection of her backside. Amanda shook her head. "I need a body double! This look would scare the fish."

Amanda looked at the suitcase with two pair of sandals and her foundation garments packed inside; then to the almost empty closet; then at the piles of clothes that had failed to make the cut strewn across the bed and every piece of furniture in the bedroom. There was little doubt in her mind that she needed a new wardrobe. She took another glance at her reflection and shuddered as she covered herself with the matching wrap skirt for the swimsuit. The thought of wearing the same swimsuit for the entire week was almost more than she could stand — especially this swimsuit. Amanda sat down at her computer and began shopping for swimsuits. Amanda went online to several sites looking for some swimsuits that would be appropriate for such an important trip. Her plan was to find one or two styles that she liked and have them delivered to the hotel they were going to stay at. Amanda found a couple of nice swimsuits that weren't too revealing and bought two of each; one the size she thought they should be and one the next size up – just to be safe.

Amanda sat on her couch with a sense of accomplishment. The swim suits, and the matching wrap skirts, should arrive at the hotel in plenty of time. She hugged the pillow as she leaned back and tucked her feet beneath her while she contemplated the trip. Even now she still found it hard to believe that she was going on a weeklong vacation with Dale Evers – alone.

From the moment she had first laid eyes on him, Amanda had felt that Dale was the man of her dreams. They had gone out on dates over the past couple of years but as far as Amanda knew they were not officially dating. On numerous occasions Amanda had tried to let Dale know how she felt about him, without being too obvious, as she waited for her turn to one day become number one in Dale's heart. Dale was a good looking man who had been so popular with the ladies that for a time he had been referred to by his coworkers as the *Playboy Diplomat.* Many of the various ambassadors' daughters had a crush on the handsome and charming man who, in the name of good international relations, would entertain their advances. While it hurt to watch Dale flirt with these girls it had soon become obvious to Amanda that this behaviour was merely a facade; a facade that Dale willingly presented to the world in an attempt to protect himself from a broken heart.

This knowledge had made it easier for Amanda to watch Dale interact with these girls, but it still hurt to have such strong feelings for a man who had, for the longest time, treated her as nothing more than a good friend. As each of the girl's advances failed to grow into anything substantial, Amanda became more hopeful that the prospect of her having a meaningful relationship with Dale was closer to becoming a reality. It gave Amanda great joy each time she was asked to check the

Will Not Attend box on the *RSVP* card in response to the numerous wedding invitations Dale received from these girls who had found the man of their dreams. However Amanda was still concerned about this one girl whose relationship with Dale was different from the others.

Amanda took a moment to think about this girl who remained a potential threat to her happiness. Consuela was both lovely and charming, and even though Dale had always acted differently towards her than the other girls, Amanda had never given it a second thought. At least she hadn't given it a second thought until the time she had done a favor for Dale's sister. Using the wedding of Consuela and Ramón as an excuse to bring Dale close enough to attend a family reunion he had no desire to be at, almost proved costly. It wasn't until the wedding had been cancelled at the last minute by Consuela that Amanda learned just how deep the feelings were between Consuela and Dale. Amanda shuddered as she thought about how close she might have come to losing Dale to Consuela, and it would have been her own fault for sending him to her.

Amanda turned back to the task at hand. She began sorting the clothes; first by what fit best and then by what she might want Dale to see her in. As she started to feel better with the clothes that were being packed in the suitcase Amanda thought about the events from earlier today that had brought her to this point. Today had started just like any other day until just before noon. This morning she had been thrilled to have Dale come to her desk and let her watch as he personally marked the RSVP card to the wedding of Consuela and Ramón. He had made sure that she had seen him mark it *Will Not Attend*, and then handed her the card and asked her to seal the envelope and mail it. Sending this letter on its way had given her more pleasure than Dale would ever know and would have been the highlight of any normal day. It was early afternoon when Dale returned to her desk and made the day even better.

Dale had come to her desk and sat on the chair in front of her for a few moments before he started to speak. "Amanda, I have a question for you."

The expression on his face had been different than normal, almost as if the question he was about to ask was going to cause him great pain. Amanda had placed the telephone receiver on her desk so they wouldn't be disturbed when it rang and had given Dale her full attention. "Hopefully I have an answer for you."

Dale had been uneasy and he began to shift in the chair while he wrung his hands. He had made good eye contact, but not with the confidence he normally showed. He licked his lips and then swallowed hard. "Good because I think that I might have done something bad."

Amanda's curiosity had been aroused as to what this boy scout of a man could have possibly done to cause this behavior. "What did you do?"

Dale had looked around to check that no one was listening and confirm that his words would stay between the two of them. He leaned towards her and spoke just above a whisper. "Without asking for your permission I have arranged some time off for both of us; reserved the flights and separate hotel rooms for a weeklong vacation in paradise." He paused. "Now I need to know if you would care to join me."

The exhilaration she had felt when the invitation was made returned every time she thought about that moment. Amanda shifted in her chair; even now she still couldn't believe how quickly she had said yes to Dale's invitation. Perhaps she should have played hard to get and kept him in suspense while she made him wait for her answer. Perhaps, but she didn't make him wait because she wasn't going to risk giving Dale time to have second thoughts and change his mind. She was going to have Dale all to herself for a whole week.

Since accepting Dale's invitation Amanda had become obsessed with the place on earth that was so dear to Dale's heart. She had been there several times in an official capacity and had thought that it was a nice place, but nothing more. But since their conversation this afternoon it meant a whole lot more to her because if it was a special place to Dale it was going to be special for her. In the short time she had been home, before trying on the entire contents of her closet, Amanda had changed her computer screen saver to a picture of the beautiful island paradise.

Amanda sat in front of her computer and admired the view and had to concede that it was definitely an island she wouldn't mind being stranded on – especially if it happened to be with Dale. She clicked a few keys to close her computer and soon had pen in hand making an entry into her journal before returning the clothes strewn across the bed to the closet and retiring for the evening.

Amanda took a moment to look at the picture of Dale she kept on her desk. She smiled when she thought of how he might blush if he knew that she had taken the picture; and then had it framed. Amanda concluded her journal entry. *Dale has always been a perfect gentleman. Today he invited me to join him in paradise. The only thing that could make this week together more perfect would be if we were there on our honeymoon.* She sat silent a few moments and continued writing. *It's a nice thought but that means Dale would need to propose.* She carefully placed the piece of ribbon in a protector sleeve that she used as a book mark and closed her journal.

Dale Evers was exhausted after a long eventful day but he still couldn't sleep. He kept reliving the highlights of his day. He remembered the joy on Amanda's face when he marked the RSVP to Ramón and Consuela's wedding as *Will Not Attend* in front of her. He smiled as he thought about how quickly she sealed the envelope and placed it in the outgoing mail bin. He then thought about their conversation later in the day when he had been so suave and debonair in inviting her to spend a week with him in paradise.

The excitement he had felt when hearing Amanda say yes to the trip he had planned was still as vivid as it had been when she had said those magical words. "Yes I would love to." He had thought that she would have answered him quicker than she did, but figured that she must have been playing hard to get.

Dale lay in his bed trying to make himself go to sleep but to no avail, there were too many happy thoughts on his mind. He reached over and turned on the small light beside his bed before he opened the night stand drawer. Dale reached into the drawer and removed a tiny velvet box which he held a few moments before opening the lid to reveal the shiny token of his love for Amanda. As the light reflected in a dazzling display off of the many facets of the diamonds in the ring set, Dale shook his head because he couldn't stop thinking of Beth.

Beth was an older lady who had worked in the office and was like a mother to everyone. After he had returned from the Christmas family reunion and the first failed attempt by Ramón and Consuela to find wedded bliss, Dale knew that he wanted to make Amanda his but was still unable to take the next step. It was at this time of uncertainty on how to proceed that Beth had come into his office uninvited and closed the door firmly behind her. Dale could still remember the intense look in her eyes when she had sat down across the desk from him and began to scold him. Beth had scolded him for several things but the main focus was his insensitivity for Amanda's feelings because of how long he had kept Amanda wondering if he would ever propose. Then in the matter of fact manner Beth was known for, she told him to do the right thing and propose to Amanda or let her get on with her life without him. Then Beth informed him that they were going to the jewelry store that very moment to buy the ring that would be worn forever on Amanda's finger - as Mrs. Dale Evers.

Dale rubbed the ring against his cheek as he remembered what had happened next. Once inside the jewelry store Dale remembered how he had turned right and went straight to the display case of wedding rings he had admired on numerous occasions. He must have gone to that display case more than he thought he had because the sales girl came over and removed the rings he normally asked to look at, without being asked. Beth had followed him to the display case and stood at his side. She agreed that the ring sets Dale was looking at were nice, but then informed him that those rings were totally inappropriate considering the situation he had created for himself. Beth had then taken the rings from his hand and returned them to the sales girl as she stated in a matter of fact tone of voice. "These are definitely lovely ring sets and at one time, had you been smart, would have done nicely."

Dale had watched the rings being returned to the display case and then turned to Beth. "Why are they not acceptable now?"

The motherly tone had returned to Beth's voice as she placed a hand on his. "You have good taste in rings and had you proposed to Amanda when we all thought that you should have, these rings would have been fine."

"What do you mean?"

Beth had reached out and rubbed Dales' cheek and then his forehead. "You are a silly boy. When you should have proposed to Amanda, you never had to shave as often as you do now and your hairline hadn't started to recede." She looked him squarely in the eye. "Are you the only one who can't see the way Amanda has looked at you since she first met you? You have taken Amanda for granted way too long and now you really need to show how much you love her, and at the same time say that you are sorry for making her wait so long."

"And how am I supposed to do that?"

Beth had motioned for him to follow as she started to walk to the expensive side of the store and stopped at a display case that made the sales girl smile. "One of these will do nicely."

Dale remembered hesitating and then hearing the next wise words from Beth.

"If you wait much longer you will need to shop for rings in the next display case. The price of those rings makes these ones look like a bargain."

Dale had selected a ring that met with Beth's approval and was relieved to find the price was one of the lowest in that display case. To this day Dale was certain that he had heard his credit card cry when the transaction was made.

The diamond engagement ring and matching wedding band were nestled safely in the box and still looked as beautiful as they did the day he first brought the rings home – all those months earlier. Dale knew that the engagement ring should be on Amanda's finger by now and he silently scolded himself for taking so long to propose. He knew it wasn't normal but every time Dale tried to say the words he hoped Amanda was waiting to hear, he would hesitate, thinking something about the moment wasn't right.

Once again Dale thought of Beth and her parting words to him as she left his office on the day she retired.

"I had hoped to see the engagement ring on Amanda's finger before I retired. I can only hope that you propose to that girl before she is old enough to retire."

Dale placed the ring on the end of his index finger and gently kissed the band. He smiled. "This time I couldn't have picked a more perfect setting for a marriage proposal." He kissed the band a second time. "When we return from my island paradise this ring will be on Amanda's finger." It was hard for him to contain his excitement as he thought about the flight, the limousine, the hotel and the beach – but best of all he was going to be with Amanda.

Dale picked up the travel brochure and smiled as he looked at the cover. The small bench beside the majestic clock tower in the town square held his gaze. This picture perfect setting would be part of their memories forever. Just as the last noon hour chime from the clock tower was fading into history, he would drop to one knee as they sat on that very bench and declare his love to the most wonderful girl in the world. He placed the ring into the nightstand drawer, turned out the light, pulled the covers around his neck, and once again tried to fall asleep. Then the phone rang.

CHAPTER ONE

Dale was relieved that the high school girls seated behind him on the airplane had finally stopped their incessant chatter and had gone to sleep. He was grateful to have a break from hearing the overused phrases that have now become his least favorite; and the next time a girl says - gag me - he just might do it.

The trip had been quite eventful and Dale was exhausted from the lack of sleep. He looked forward to reaching his destination and planned on making full use of the bed in his room after checking into the hotel. It was late and his body craved sleep. Being awake at this hour was insane since there was no logical reason for anyone other than the flight attendants to be up, yet he was still awake. Dale had always been envious at how easy it was for Amanda to fall asleep in an airplane while travelling on their trips. He yawned and closed his eyes as he tried to make himself go to sleep. It had only been a few minutes before he opened his eyes again after hearing the soft chime sound from the console above his head. The *Fasten Seat Belt* light had been illuminated. Dale checked his seatbelt and then buckled it; he then checked the seatbelt for the seat next to him and then closed his eyes.

Any thoughts Dale had entertained about sleeping were gone when the plane dropped several feet and veered hard to the right in a sharp descent. Panicked screams were heard as a lightning flash illuminated the cabin. Each subsequent lightening flash and deafening thunder clap brought a hysterical cry from the girl seated next to him. When the plane was below the storm and started flying level again the grip on his arm was released which allowed the blood flow to return to his fingers. Dale wiped the tears from the girl's face and in a soft calm voice tried to reassure her. "Everything is going to be alright. The plane is flying much more smoothly now."

The airplane gave another small shudder just before the pilot's voice came over the speakers. "Ladies and gentlemen everything is under control. We are out of the storm and we have received permission from ground control to change altitude and alter our course so that we can fly around the storm. Our cabin crew will tend to your needs so please sit back and relax while you enjoy the rest of the flight."

Moments later the pilot's voice returned. "Ladies and gentlemen I am happy to report that even with our course change we will be arriving at our destination in less than two hours and will be only thirty eight minutes behind schedule."

Dale rubbed his eyes and suppressed a yawn. He laid his head against the head rest and looked out of the cabin window. He watched the darkness begin to dissipate as the rising sun colored the clouds on the horizon with brilliant hues of red and yellow.

The girl beside him was doing much better so Dale helped her look out of the window to see the sunrise. As she looked at the colorful display Dale told her, "When you see a sunrise with colors like that after a storm it will be a good day." Dale admired the sunrise a few minutes more and had to admit that of the two sunrises he had been privileged to witness during this trip, this one was the most impressive.

A strained smile came to his face as he remembered the pilot saying they would be thirty eight minutes late in arriving. To be only thirty eight minutes behind schedule on this trip would be a welcome treat. When the flight arrived, if it arrived when the pilot said it would, Dale's travel time would be twenty six hours longer than his original travel plans.

Watching the beautiful sight of gentle waves lapping at the miles of near empty beaches in the early morning light brought a tear to Dale's eye. A quick glance at his watch confirmed that the time was well past when he had planned to be down on one knee by the majestic bell tower proposing to Amanda.

As the sun rose past the horizon in the morning sky, Dale thought about the events that had changed his plans from a week in paradise with Amanda to a work assignment on the other side of the world. Dale still resented that early morning phone call when his supervisor informed him about a developing situation that only he could handle; and that his trip to paradise with Amanda would have to wait.

Dale tried to quell his growing resentment for this difficult man but it was no use as once again his feelings of frustration returned. It seemed that from the first time this supervisor had come into his life, there was one roadblock after another to any advancement and promotion for Dale in his chosen career; and now it seemed that this evil man was looking to find enjoyment messing with Dale's personal life.

Dale tried to put the supervisor out of his thoughts but couldn't. This man had been associated with every recent disappointment in his life. Dale was angry to think that one minute he had been lying in bed hugging his pillow while dreaming about the perfect marriage proposal to Amanda he had planned; followed by a long walk on the beach and then a romantic dinner in the finest restaurant in town to celebrate their engagement. Only to find that the next minute he was faced with the harsh reality that his plans had been changed and his week in paradise with Amanda was on hold indefinitely. His frustration with the new development had become even worse when the supervisor told him that he had to inform Amanda of the change of plans, and then ask her to book his new flights so that he could attend the wedding of Ramón and Consuela.

Dale remembered every uncomfortable detail of that conversation. He had assured Amanda that attending the wedding of Ramón and Consuela was not his idea. He had explained to her that attending the wedding was an assignment and nothing more. He wished that he could have mentioned to her the part about an unknown situation arising that only he could handle, but he had been instructed not to tell Amanda anything about what was happening. The answers he had given Amanda though lacking in detail were the truth and Dale thought that they had sounded good.

Amanda on the other hand had seemed less than convinced with the explanation. Dale remembered how visibly hurt and upset Amanda had been when she left his office to book the flights. The only words she had spoken to him since that conversation in his office were when she handed him the tickets. Even then she spoke only enough to inform him that the first scheduled flight was not the one he normally took since all the other flights were already booked. Her smile had been warm but a bit disconcerting when she assured him that this flight would connect with his regular flight before crossing the ocean.

Dale reviewed the adventures of his trip and wondered if Amanda had booked the trip the way she did to teach him a lesson, but he wondered for just a brief moment. Just as fast as the thought had entered his mind he felt a twinge of guilt for even thinking that Amanda would do something like that. Either way, so far this trip had been quite an adventure with missed connections, cancelled flights, and up to this point his favorite was still the delayed flight when the runway had been taken over by a herd of ill tempered camels.

Back at the office Amanda felt bad about the flights she had booked and her behaviour towards Dale before he had left for the wedding. She was concerned that Dale had yet to call and let her know that he had arrived safely at his destination. She was becoming even more concerned that the reason he hadn't called her was because he might be upset with the choice of flights. The first flight she had booked was with a small local airline that used small planes with cargo nets for seats and usually allowed animals to be in the cabin with their owners, she wondered if the choices she made out of frustration may have been too much. Her concern for Dale grew with each passing minute that the phone never rang. Amanda couldn't decide what had made her act the way she did. She wondered if it was her jealousy towards Consuela and her relationship with Dale; or if it was the disappointment of losing out on a week in paradise with Dale that had made her cross the line with her choice of Dale's flights and connections.

Almost three hours from the pilot's announcement that they would be approximately thirty eight minutes late in arriving, Dale was waiting at the luggage carousel for his bags. The cumulative lack of sleep from his trip was taking its toll as it was a constant battle for Dale to keep his eyes open. Since catching the first flight of this unexpected adventure Dale had only managed to catch a couple of hours sleep at best. Never before had he been so blessed to be in the company of so many passengers on his flights who never quit talking – ever. He had been unable to sleep during the several lengthy layovers and delays either. The airports he had been in were notorious for personal belongings going missing from weary travelers who dosed off briefly, and he wasn't about to let that happen to him.

Dale made his way through the busy airport terminal and checked his bags with the airline for his next flight. Wandering around the terminal his attention was drawn to the newscast on the television but the volume was so low that he had to stand in front of the screen and strain to hear the story behind the footage. Just as he was close enough to hear what the news anchor was saying, a child beside him started talking and made it impossible to understand anything that was being said. This child was voicing her displeasure about something in a language other than English and Dale tried to ignore her. Moments later Dale felt a sharp stinging pain in his right ankle. The pain made Dale drop to one knee and grab the painful joint with both hands. While he was clutching his ankle he found himself looking into the eyes of a determined young girl who stood there glaring at him. Dale had no idea who the girl was and why she had kicked him. He never had a chance to find out who she was and why she had kicked him as the child ran away and disappeared into the crowded terminal.

With the last flight being so late arriving it was no surprise to Dale that his connecting flight had already left and any spaces on any of the other available flights were already taken. Dale bought a bottle of cold water and placed it against his throbbing ankle as he took a seat and waited for his next flight.

This latest delay was just another inconvenience in an already inconvenient trip but at least now he was able to watch the newscast uninterrupted. The images that flashed on the screen were unsettling for Dale as he watched the beautiful tall ships in the harbour vanish from view behind a thick dense cloud of black smoke. Even more unsettling to Dale was being able to watch the explosion originate from the bench in the main square, near the majestic clock tower, just as the final chime marking the noon hour faded into history. Dale watched in disbelief. As the video clip played over and over Dale felt numb with the knowledge that if he wasn't going to Consuela's wedding; he would have been on one knee proposing to Amanda, at the exact time and place where the bomb went off.

Dale wanted to hear Amanda's voice; he wanted to speak with her just to know that she was safe. He debated if he should call and wake her in the middle of the night. As the video clip started to play again he reached for his phone. Before he could dial her number the announcement came over the speakers that his next flight was about to board. Considering how things had been going so far, Dale felt that he should be at the front of the line so that he wouldn't be bumped again on the same trip.

As the plane flew over the familiar landmarks that showed Dale that his journey was coming to an end, Dale was so exhausted that it was all he could do to stay awake. Dale breathed a sigh of relief when the plane arrived at the terminal and they had unloaded the plane. No more flights to catch.

At the baggage pick up area Dale was able to grab his bags with relative ease but was shocked to find that his cart had been taken over by the elderly couple standing next to him while his attention was focused on finding his bags. This couple had swiftly removed his carryon bag and set it on the floor next to him; loaded their bags onto the cart and left as fast as they could, leaving Dale standing with his bags and no cart. He struggled with his bags until he was able to find another cart and then made his way to customs. Once he had cleared customs and was in the main part of the terminal, Dale removed his cell phone from the inner pocket of his suit coat and was going to call Amanda before he did anything else.

Dale turned on his phone and briefly saw the picture of the battery with a thin red line just before the phone turned off. Dale stood in the terminal looking at his phone; wondering how he could have been so foolish to pass the time between flights playing all those silly games. He should have preserved the battery for an emergency which this now was since all of the numbers he needed were locked inside of this compact electronic jail.

Dale put the phone back into his pocket and took a deep breath to help clear his mind. He smiled when he realised that all was not lost. He may not have access to the phone numbers for his reservations but he knew what to do. He placed his carryon bag over his shoulder and grabbed the handles of his other bags, the ones with the broken wheels that wouldn't roll properly. It required a lot of effort and concentration for Dale to pull the bags as he tried to walk and protect his sore right ankle while he limped away from the terminal. He had almost made his way to the first cab in taxi row when he was pushed aside by a rather portly lady with a large entourage rushing towards the cab, and the next three in line. Dale stopped himself from falling over his bags and was about to say something not dignified of a diplomat when the sharp pain in his ankle brought him to one knee.

Dale was in obvious discomfort as he checked to make sure that his ankle would support his weight before trying to continue walking any further. He reached for the handles of his bags and struggled to pull them before a taxi driver took the bags from him and loaded them into the cab. The driver opened the door and helped Dale into the cab. Dale was glad to be seated and gave a sigh of relief. Dale told the driver his destination before he laid his head against the seat back and tried to ignore the throbbing in his ankle.

Dale saw the limousine from the Mexican Embassy parked in another line as they pulled away from the curb and wondered if Ramón was going to be the passenger. Before Dale's taxi had even left the airport, Dale was fast asleep. The taxi came to an abrupt stop in front of Gail's house which roused Dale from a sound sleep. He paid the driver then gingerly climbed out of the taxi and waited for his bags to be unloaded.

Dale placed the strap of his carryon bag over his shoulder, gathered his broken luggage, and then tested his ankle as he prepared for the long walk up the winding walkway to the front door. He had only taken a few painful steps before his attention was drawn back towards the road. He had heard the soft chirp of car brakes followed by the sound of a car door closing.

A hand joined his on the bag handles. "Let me help you with your bags Senor Evers."

Dale surrendered his grip on the handles and turned his head towards the person. "What brings you here Eduard? Don't you have passengers to deliver?"

Eduard accompanied Dale to the end of the walk where they stopped at the front door and rang the bell. "I have already been to the embassy with my passengers."

Dale was a little perplexed at how Eduard had been able to make the drive to the Mexican Embassy to drop off his passengers and make it there in the time it took for the short drive to his sister's house from the airport. "How did you make it here so quickly?"

Eduard smiled. "It has been over an hour since I left the airport with my passengers and took them to the embassy. I think that maybe your driver took the scenic route when you may have dozed off."

Dale wondered how Eduard knew that he may have dozed off but figured it out when the driver smiled and pointed to the corner of his own mouth and wiped at it with the tip of his index finger. Dale wiped at his own mouth and could feel the small crusty buildup. He figured that the design of the cabs interior was probably imprinted on the side of his face as well. As Dale became more awake and thought about it, he realized that he had paid a lot more than normal for a drive that should only take twenty five minutes.

"Thank you for helping me with my bags Eduard. But why are you here?"

Before the question could be answered Gail opened the door. "Dale, this is an unexpected surprise. Why didn't you tell me you were coming?" Gail looked at Eduard, and then at the car on the front street with small flags on the fenders, and then back to Dale. "Are you in town for Consuela's wedding?" Her question was interrupted when she saw the condition Dale was in. Here was her brother, the king of must always look good, sporting an impressive growth of facial hair; looking and smelling like he had been sleeping in his clothes under a bridge with livestock, if he had even slept at all. Gail stepped aside. "Where are my manners? Please come in."

Dale winced as he stepped forward and hoped that Gail hadn't noticed. It became obvious that Gail had seen his limp as she watched his every step with a look of concern. He was surprised when Gail never made a big deal about his limp and turned her attention to directing Eduard where to place the bags.

"So Eduard did you meet Dale at the airport to bring him here?"

Eduard glanced at Dale before he answered. "No I did not. I have been sent to your home at the request of the Ambassador to bring Dale to the embassy as quickly as possible."

Dale yawned as he rubbed his face and scratched at the facial hair. "How did he even know that I was in town?"

Eduard smiled. "I told him that I had seen you at the airport when you were pushed onto your bags by that large lady and her friends."

Gail reached to lift Dale's pant leg and expose the swollen ankle. "A lady pushed you to the ground? Are you hurt?"

"I'll be fine sis." Dale pulled the fabric from Gail's hand and turned to Eduard. "Why does the ambassador need me at the embassy right now?"

Eduard looked at Dale. "When I told him that I had seen you at the airport he sent me to bring you to him immediately."

Dale yawned and his shoulders drooped slightly with the prospect of sleep once again in jeopardy. As he dutifully turned to join Eduard, Gail grabbed his arm. She held her nose and then pointed into the house. "You need a shower before you go anywhere and I strongly recommend changing into clothes that smell better than a barnyard." Gail pulled the suit jacket from his shoulders. "If you are really lucky the drycleaner can salvage your suit, otherwise I may just have to burn it."

CHAPTER TWO

*D*ale felt like a new man after enjoying a long overdue shower and taking care of some basic needs of hygiene that had been neglected during the trip. Now that the film was gone from his teeth and he was shaved, showered and clean, Dale could detect the offensive smell of his clothes and could only imagine what all of those people unfortunate enough to be confined on the plane with him must have thought. When Dale finished dressing he looked in the mirror and was pleased to see that the scraggly wreck had been transformed into a respectable looking member of society. Dale wanted to be sure that he smelled as good as he looked and applied a second splash of cologne for good measure before he left the room.

The subtle fragrance reminded him of Amanda since it was a gift from her and she always commented on how nice that cologne smelled when he wore it. He wanted to call Amanda before leaving for the embassy but he knew that there wasn't enough time for the conversation he wanted to have. Oh how he wanted to hear her voice. He wanted to know that things between them were still good and that she was doing okay. He wanted to thank Amanda for her thoughtfulness in planning the trip. He wanted to share his relief that their trip had been postponed and that they were nowhere near the bombing, but then remembered that she had no idea just how close they would have been to disaster. Dale picked up his phone and when it failed to come to life was reminded that it needed to be charged. Dale rummaged in his bag for the charger and eventually had the phone charging on the end table.

Dale ran his fingers through his hair and looked in the mirror a final time. He checked for things between his teeth, and then at the dark circles and bags under his eyes. He confirmed that his phone was charging so he could call Amanda when he returned, and then went downstairs.

Dale made his way to the bottom of the stairs and waited for Gail to declare him fit to be in the company of others.

Gail gave him a hug and breathed deeply. "Now you look and smell good enough to be in public." She paused. "So where did you leave your dirty clothes?"

"I left them in the room."

Gail had a concerned look. "You didn't leave your dirty clothes on my new bedspread did you?"

Dale thought a few moments before he turned and limped towards the stairs. "Where would you like me to put them?"

Gail placed her hand on his arm to stop him. "Don't bother; Amber will take care of the clothes. I think that you need to go." Gail called Amber. "Amber will you please get Uncle Dale's clothes from his room and bring them to me."

"Uncle Dales is here?" Amber entered the room and gave Dale a big hug around the legs before she stepped away to stand beside Gail. She looked at Eduard and then around the room. "Why didn't you bring Amanda with you?"

"She had to work." Dale felt that he had answered poorly as he watched Amber's expression change.

Gail placed her hands on Amber's shoulders. "You need to hurry and get Uncle Dale's clothes off of the bed before the smell becomes permanent in the new bed spread."

Amber stared at Dale in a way similar to how the little girl from the airport had looked at him. "You should have brought Amanda." Dale stepped back as if to get out of the reach of Amber's feet.

Gail turned Amber towards the stairs. "You need to get the clothes right now."

Amber sighed and went to Dale's room.

Once Amber was out of sight Dale immediately motioned for Eduard to join him as he left the house. It was obvious that Amber was in Dale's room when they heard. "E-e-e-w-w! These clothes stink!"

Dale could feel the need for sleep once again taking over as he sat in the limousine but kept awake by speaking with Eduard. Dale had hoped that during their conversation he would be able to find even the smallest clue as to why it was so urgent for him to be at the embassy. Eduard was as professional as they come and Dale realised that this man knew how to keep a secret. By the end of the ride Dale was no closer to knowing the urgency behind why his presence was needed at the embassy, but at least he was still awake.

Dale was escorted to the ambassador's office. Before any conversation began the door was closed firmly behind them. "Dale, we have a situation."

"Isn't that why I am here?" Dale hobbled to the chair the ambassador offered him, sat down and then lightly rubbed his swollen ankle. "What is the situation that brings me to the wedding?" Dale attempted to lighten the mood. "Has Ramón done something to upset Consuela before he has even arrived?"

The ambassador turned on the large flat screen monitor and pressed play on the video player. "Ramón not being here has just created a situation, and I fear that it could be serious."

Dale watched a recording from the security feed showing the front drive and the road outside of the embassy where Ramón was stationed. He watched Ramón and his best man enter the limousine; he then followed the path of the limousine as the driver pulled through the gate and onto the road. The feed then switched to a street surveillance camera. Dale watched the vehicle travel to an intersection that was almost out of view when something unexpected happened. The limousine was blocked when a delivery truck came to an abrupt stop in the middle of the intersection. A car then pulled up behind the limousine to block it from the rear, and then a van pulled alongside the limousine. With military precision, armed masked men pulled Ramón and his friend from the back seat of the limousine and forced them into the open side door of the van before it sped away.

The large screen went dark and the two men sat in silence. Dale was in a state of disbelief at what had just played out before his eyes. He knew from past incidents of a similar nature in that part of the world that this was a potentially serious situation Ramón was in. Dale was a diplomat by profession and knew how he should have responded to this situation and felt that his actions may have seemed disrespectful when he was unable to stifle a big yawn. "Has there been any ransom demand?"

The ambassador wrung his hands as he spoke. "It has been three days and we have not been contacted with any ransom demand. In fact there has been no contact made since this incident happened." The ambassador had a worried look on his face.

The silence was awkward as Dale studied the man across the room from him. The last politically motivated abductions in that country had not ended well and Dale could only wonder what the ambassador was thinking.

There were a couple of deep breaths and a controlled sigh before the ambassador spoke. "We have no idea why this would have happened and what to think about it, all we can do is wait and hope for the best." The ambassador paused and looked intently at Dale. "What I need you to do is pretend that everything is fine and keep Consuela calm. She has been quite concerned since Ramón's flight landed and he wasn't on it. She has been unable to contact him and fears that something bad has happened."

"So Consuela has no idea what has happened?" Dale waited for an answer he felt he already knew. He was certain that if Consuela knew Ramón was in trouble she would have already called him.

The ambassador hung his head. "No, Consuela knows nothing about what has happened to keep Ramón from being with her."

Dale wondered about the secrecy surrounding Ramón's disappearance and why Consuela would not be told about it. "Why not just tell Consuela the truth about what happened?"

In a hushed voice the ambassador answered. "I know that I should tell Consuela what has happened but it is not that simple."

"What is so difficult about telling your daughter the truth?"

The Ambassador replayed the video. "I would have told Consuela the moment I found out about Ramón but I do not wish to risk having Ramón's family find out what has happened until I have an answer for them. They would all take turns bothering me for an update that I don't have, and then insist that I give them one."

Dale was silent as he determined his response that in the end was no different than his first response. "I still think Consuela deserves to know the truth about the situation with Ramón."

The ambassador wrung his hands. "I agree with you, but I can't risk telling her just yet." He looked intently at Dale. "You need to help me keep her calm, but not let her know what has happened."

Dale cared a great deal for Consuela and didn't like the idea of keeping secrets from her, but he had been given a directive and would do as he had been told. The moment the door to the office opened Dale was joined by security as he made his way to Consuela's room. He stopped outside the door. Dale started to reach for the door to knock but instead of tapping on the door he let his hand fall to his side. The uncertainty he felt in his heart at the prospects of seeing Consuela was real. The very reason for not wanting to attend the wedding was to avoid these feelings welling up in his heart. He loved Amanda and wanted to marry her, but there were still unresolved feelings for Consuela which seemed to be heightened when mixed in with concern over the current situation with Ramón. The security detail was getting restless as he stood in front of the door and Dale knew that he had to act. The feeling associated with this situation felt very familiar to the ones he felt at the last almost wedding as Dale reached up and knocked on the door in his special way. "Consuela it's me, Dale; could you please open the door?"

There was a pause. Finally the door opened a crack. Consuela had a look of surprise on her face as she invited Dale into the room but never showed herself to the others waiting near the door. Dale entered and the door was closed firmly behind him. Consuela gave Dale a hug. "What are you doing here? I thought that you were not able to come to my wedding?"

Dale was uncomfortable as he felt emotions begin to rise in his heart before he pulled away from the familiar warmth of Consuela's hug and held her by the hands. Dale knew what he should say but something inside made him hesitate slightly before giving his reply. "I was unable to come until there was a change of plans that kept Amanda from joining me for a week on a tropical Island where I was going to propose to her, so here I am."

Consuela looked at Dale. "I am so sorry that things never worked out for you and Amanda. But I am glad to have you here for my wedding. Ramón will be so surprised to see you when he arrives."

Dale felt a surge of different emotions rise within his heart as he remembered being told to come to the wedding instead of being with Amanda. He composed himself before responding. "I'm glad that I can be here for you."

Consuela turned from Dale to look out of the window. "Ramón will be so happy to see you when he gets here."

Dale watched this beautiful young woman look off into the distance from her bedroom window without saying a word for the longest time. Each time she would glance over at him he could see the tears forming in her eyes before she would look away. "Consuela, what is going on?"

Consuela's behavior continued for several minutes before she finally broke down in tears. "Something has happened to keep Ramón from being here. I can feel it in my heart."

Dale feigned a look of surprise. "What would make you say that something has happened to Ramón?" He didn't know how convincing his performance was but he knew that he had to continue. Dale paused momentarily as he resisted the urge to take her in his arms to console her. "When was Ramón supposed to arrive?"

Consuela lowered her head and covered her face with her hands as she began to sob. "I thought that he would have been here with his best man the day before yesterday."

Dale didn't want to upset Consuela any further and thought that he could soften the reality of the situation. "Maybe Ramón is having problems with his flights like I did with mine."

"Do you really think so?"

Dale smiled as he took Consuela by the hand. "It's possible he is having unexpected travel delays like I did. I had things happen to me on my flights that I never would have believed possible until now, and I still made it here for the wedding. Give him more time. He will be here." Dale hoped that his words would comfort her. They seemed to have worked for a moment.

Consuela looked at Dale with teary eyes. "Then why has he not called me?"

Dale saw the look of concern returning and knew that he had to say something to alleviate the fears. "He probably ran out of battery playing games on his phone like I did during my trip and has to recharge it before he can call you."

Consuela lowered her eyes and then laughed as she moved to the window. "The way Ramón plays games on his phone you could be right about the battery going dead." After a few moments she began to relax. She had no solid news to support her concern, but it was obvious that she was still very concerned.

Dale moved across the room to join Consuela at the window as he resisted the urge to sleep. His ankle hurt so when he took the first step his limp and discomfort were more noticeable than he had hoped.

Consuela showed concern for Dale's discomfort. "Did you hurt yourself coming to my wedding?"

Dale showed great restraint in not expressing his true feelings for the condition of his ankle and smiled as he pointed out of the window toward the garden. "Who is that adorable little girl I see in the garden?"

Consuela looked to where he was pointing. "Are you pointing at the girl in the blue dress or the red dress?"

Dale tried not to be too obvious who he was pointing at and looked away. "I'm asking about the girl in the blue dress who is now staring at us."

"That would be one of my bridesmaids, Ramón's niece Cecelia." Consuela waved at the girl who had stopped playing and stared intently at Dale and Consuela standing at the window. She broke her stare long enough to smile and wave at Consuela, but then folded her arms and scowled as she glared at Dale.

"I don't think she likes you." Consuela joked as she gently nudged Dale's ribs.

Dale moved away from the window. "I would get that impression."

"So tell me what happened to your leg?"

Without any hesitation Dale motioned towards the garden. "Cecelia."

"Cecelia?"" Consuela had a puzzled expression that slowly turned into a horrified look as Dale raised his pant leg and she saw Dale's badly bruised and swollen ankle.

Dale let the pant legs fall back into place. "She introduced herself to me at an airport along the way."

Consuela looked at the innocent looking young lady playing in the garden with the other children and gently shook her head. "That Cecelia can really hold a grudge."

Dale was surprised to hear Consuela mention the word grudge in referring to Cecelia "How can she possibly hold a grudge against me? As far as I know, we have never met before today."Dale waited for an answer, an answer which eventually came between snickers and small bouts of laughter.

"You have met before. Cecelia blames you for her not being a flower girl at the last wedding."

"What did I do?"

Consuela explained the situation and revealed why Dale was public enemy number one. "Ramón's sister doesn't believe that you were there to comfort me after I sent Ramón away last time. She thinks it was because of you, that I sent Ramón and my bridesmaids away. Cecelia loves her mother and believes what she has been told."

"That would explain a lot."Dale could still see the concern on Consuela's face as they talked about Ramón but was glad that she was becoming more relaxed. When Dale was unable to control his yawning and started to doze off in the middle of a sentence, Eduard was summoned to return Dale home.

Ramón Ramirez came out of the water and crossed the sand to his lounge chair and dried himself with a towel. He motioned to the attendant for another drink and turned to watch the girls playing beach volleyball. Ramón had always dreamed about having a bachelor party at an exotic location like this but never thought that it would ever happen – until now. His dream had been fulfilled thanks to the thoughtful planning of his best man.

CHAPTER THREE

*D*ales' return to Gail's house was greeted by Gail and Amber, who both had a myriad of questions which it seemed they felt couldn't wait to be answered. Dale made them wait until the next morning to ask their questions as he went straight to his room without stopping to visit.

After a good night's rest which lasted well past noon, Dale was able to think more clearly. The first thing on his mind to do was call Amanda. He reached for his phone and saw that it was where he had left it, but noticed that it wasn't plugged into the charger. Dale was certain that he had plugged it in before he left for the embassy but conceded that in his sleep deprived state might have forgotten to plug it in. But if he had forgotten to plug it in how did the charger get plugged into the wall?

When Dale finally picked up his phone he turned it on to find it had less than ten percent charge. That meant that it must have been plugged in at one point, but why was it not plugged in now? He slid his thumb across the screen to unlock the phone and a smile came to his face. The game he had loaded onto his phone for Amber to play when he was here on his last visit was open. He touched the screen to close the game but instead his thumb hit the icon to start the next level, a level which he had almost mastered the last time he played it with Amber. Instead of turning off the game to make the call he couldn't resist the challenge and tried to see if he could be victorious and gain bragging rights when he saw Amber. Thirteen tries later Dale had failed to win the level but he had to quit when his phone had shut down.

Dale hung his head as he realized what he had just done and laughed as he reached to plug the phone onto the charger.

Gail entered the room while he was laughing. "Amanda called earlier and I tried to wake you, but failed. You must have been really tired. Anyway I told her that I would have you call when you woke up." She watched him plug his phone onto the charger. "You can use the phone in the den. Speed dial number five is her number at work, but if she isn't there use speed dial number six for her home phone."

"Thank you for the message." Dale paused. "Why would she call here? Staying here wasn't part of the trip."

"Amanda was worried when you hadn't called her and you still hadn't checked into the hotel she had booked. She called here to see if I knew anything about where you were or if something bad had happened to you." Gail paused. "She also asked if I thought that you might be upset with her."

Dale went thoughtful. "I wonder why she would ask that."

Gail looked intently at her brother. "Is there something that I should be aware of for the next time Amanda calls?"

Dale shrugged. "Not that I can think of. I'll call her and see what is happening." Dale went to the den, the whole time trying to decide which number to use. It was at that time of day where she could be at either location. He decided to try her at home first. If she was there they would have more time to talk. Dale was excited by the prospects of speaking with Amanda but the feelings he had felt the night before with Consuela slowed his hand as he reached for the phone. As the number dialed and the phone began to ring he thought how strange it was for Gail to have Amanda on speed dial. After the seventh ring he was ready to push the release button when a voice came on the phone.

"Hello?"

To hear Amanda say that simple word was all Dale needed to calm his troubled heart. "Hi Amanda, it's Dale, how are you doing?"

"I'm doing fine. How was your trip?"

Dale knew what he thought about the trip but didn't want to spoil the moment so he was the perfect gentleman when he responded. "Once I made the connection with the overseas flight it was smooth sailing."

Amanda gave a sigh of relief. "Oh that's good." There was a moment of silence before she spoke again. "Have you heard the news?"

The only thing Dale had been aware of during his trip was the bombing but he wasn't about to guess at what Amanda was going to say. "What news?"

"We have a new person in the office as a temporary replacement for you while you are away."

The news caught Dale by surprise since he was only away attending a wedding. He thought about the development a few moments and shrugged it off. "So, does my temporary replacement wear high heels or hiking boots?"

Amanda was silent a few moments before she responded. "What kind of question is that?"

Dale loved saying things to catch Amanda off guard. "Well, does he wear hiking boots or does she wear high heels?"

Amanda enjoyed this kind of conversation with Dale. "She could wear hiking boots just as well as he could wear high heels." She chuckled, "I do hope he likes hiking boots, otherwise he may have a nicer wardrobe than I do."

They shared the moment of levity before Dale's next question. "So is the replacement a man who looks like Quasimodo and is ready to retire?"

Amanda started to giggle. "You could only wish that he looked so unique." She paused. "As for his age this man might retire in thirty or so years."

They shared a laugh before Dale became more subdued and serious. "Did you hear about what happened where we were going for our vacation?"

Amanda was more sober when she replied. "Yes I did." There was a hint of emotion in her voice. "We could have been close to the bomb. It was right across the street from our hotel."

"Do they know who did it?"

Amanda spoke softly. "No one has claimed responsibility for the bombing but they did say that the damage was superficial. The bomb made more smoke than anything."

Dale was relieved to hear that the damage was minimal but he had to ask, "Would you still go there with me for a vacation?"

"Absolutely!" her voice became excited, "My bags are still packed."

Dale was happy to hear the answer because he was going to put a ring on her finger and he still felt that was the perfect place. The urge to tell Amanda how much he loved her grew in his chest, but was tempered by his belief that a tender declaration like that needed to be made in person. "Well I should let you go. I'm sure that you have lots to do and I need to be at the Embassy. Since Ramón has gone missing the uncertainty over the wedding has people on edge and emotional."

"Ramón has gone missing?"

Dale was comfortable enough talking to Amanda that he slipped up with his response. "Didn't you know about the abduction?" Dale placed a hand over his mouth and instantly felt that he had overstepped his bounds by mentioning the word abduction. The abduction was obviously being kept quiet in the diplomatic community. Dale spoke softly. "Perhaps I spoke too quickly by saying the word abduction. Ramón has failed to arrive for the wedding but he still has time to get here. So forget what I said about there being any abduction and think happy thoughts for Consuela."

Amanda sounded concerned. "You don't think that he went on one last fling that will cause Consuela to cancel the wedding do you?"

Dale felt that while Amanda sounded concerned for Ramón he was certain that her main concern was more about his relationship with Consuela than it was for the safety of Ramón. "If she does cancel the wedding I will be on the first flight home."

They finished their conversation with some small talk and said their goodbyes.

Dale took a deep breath and followed the smell of bacon to the kitchen. Amber was sitting at the table with one of her dolls in a small booster seat next to her. A sight that surprised Dale since Amber had declared that she was too old to play with dolls and requested that he not to get her any more dolls as a gift. Amber and her doll appeared to be waiting for breakfast. He greeted Gail before taking a seat across the table from Amber and watched her interaction with the doll. He smiled when Amber asked questions about him to the doll, and not directly to him. His initial thought to explain this form of indirect interrogation was that Gail must have told Amber not to ask him so many questions about what was going on in his life.

"So Cathy what do you think was going on at the embassy last night?" Amber placed some dry cereal on the table in front of Cathy and pretended to feed the doll and listen to a response before carrying the conversation. "I don't know either but it would be nice to know what happened to make Uncle Dale limp."

Gail stepped in as she placed a plate of food in front of Amber. "Is there nothing else for you and Cathy to talk about besides your Uncle Dale?"

Undaunted, Amber glanced at her mother before she continued. "Cathy, do you think that Amanda and Uncle Dale will ever get married?"

Gail placed a plate of food in front of Dale and appeared ready to say something to Amber when Dale placed a hand on her forearm. "Let the two of them talk, it's an interesting conversation, and quite enlightening."

Dale listened to Amber discussing her concerns with Cathy as he ate. Once Amber was at a loss for things to say Dale addressed the things that Amber had been discussing with Cathy. He hoped that he had learned his lessons from previous experiences and could give good answers that would satisfy Amber and not generate more questions. "If Cathy was wondering what happened to make me limp, I am pretty sure that you might be wondering the same thing."

Amber sat straight in her chair and faced Dale. "So what did happen to make you limp?"

Dale leaned close to Amber. "I was kicked by a little girl in an airport."

Amber leaned towards Cathy. "I told you he wouldn't tell us the truth."

Dale was shocked to hear the comment and started to plead his case. "Honest. The girl was about your size and kicks like a mule. I think she plays soccer."

Amber leaned towards Dale. "So why do you think the little girl kicked you?"

Dale sensed that they may be there for a while and asked Gail for a second helping of breakfast. "The girls name is Cecelia. She kicked me on the ankle because she thinks that she doesn't like me."

Amber raised an eyebrow. "What do you mean she thinks that she doesn't like you? I know when I don't like someone."

Dale knew that he hadn't been clear enough with the details in what he was telling her so he tried again. "Cecelia is Ramón's niece and she kicked me because she was disappointed that the first wedding was called off and she never got to be a flower girl. She thinks that it was because of me that the wedding was called off."

"So why did she kick you now?"

"I think that she kicked me because she thinks that if I am around Consuela this wedding might not happen, and this time instead of not being the flower girl she might not get to be a bridesmaid."

Amber was silent for a moment. "A little girl can be a bridesmaid?"

Gail took the opportunity to spare Dale and answered the question. "Sweetheart age has nothing to do with who can be a bridesmaid."

Amber began to have a secret whisper conversation with Cathy before she turned to Dale. "Can I be a bridesmaid at your wedding when you and Amanda get married?"

Dale had always known that there are times when no safe answer is available to a question or to a situation. This he felt was one of those times. Right now he could feel the tightening in his chest as he tried to envision the potential consequences of any answer he might give to his niece. The silence was awkward as Dale played the various scenarios out in his mind.

There was no way of knowing how Amber would react to any answer he might give. Having Amanda's phone numbers on speed dial was now a frightening thought. Amber knew how to use the phone and could call Amanda to ask that very question without anyone's knowledge. Dale thought that he might have found a loophole to avoid giving a direct answer, but then thought better of using it when he realised that the loophole might become a noose.

Amber leaned over to Cathy when Dale took so long to answer. "I don't think Uncle Dale wants us to be part of his wedding."

Dale knew that he had to give Amber an answer and decided to play her game of talking to the doll as he turned towards Cathy. "I would be disappointed if you and Amber were not a part of my wedding, when there is one."

Amber pretended to listen to Cathy a few moments and then said, "Cathy wants to know why there is still no wedding announcement. Did Amanda say no when you asked her to marry you?"

The abrupt nature of the question caught Dale off guard but he chose to answer truthfully. "Amanda never said no to my proposal of marriage because I still haven't asked her to marry me."

Amber pretended to feed Cathy. "Are you afraid that Amanda will say no when you ask her to marry you?"

Dale could only wonder where Amber was coming up with these questions. He glanced at Gail who never made a sound. "I am not afraid that Amanda will say no."

This time there was no pretend conversation with Cathy as Amber looked directly into Dale's eyes. "Are you afraid that Amanda will say yes?"

The silence from Gail was broken when the question was asked. Not to offer a profound response to satisfy the curiosity of the young interrogator. The silence was broken when an uncontrolled snicker slipped out. The uncomfortable look on Dale's face had been priceless.

Before Dale could respond to the question, other questions came at him. "Why are you waiting to ask her to marry you? Amanda isn't getting any younger, right mommy?"

Dale turned his attention to Gail who was starting to glow a bright shade of red. Amber's comment had made it evident that there had been conversations about him and Amanda; most likely about the prospects of matrimony. Dale smiled and patiently waited for Gail to speak.

Gail responded but spoke very slowly as she chose her words carefully. "I never said that Amanda wasn't getting any younger waiting for you to propose. We were discussing the lack of progress in our efforts to locate her birthmother before she gets married."

Dale gave Gail a mischievous wink that Amber was unable to see. "That's all there is about the statement?"

"That's all there is." Gail was firm in her gaze towards Dale.

"All right then." Dale wanted to change the topic so he reached into his pocket and pulled out a big shiny coin that he handed to Amber. "I picked this up for your coin collection during my trip. What do you think, will it do?"

Amber gently rubbed the coin and checked it out before she looked at Dale. "Do you have any more?"

Dale pulled out a smaller coin. "This coin came from a country that I have never been to before this trip." He held it in his hand and waited for Amber to take it. "Those are the only new coins I have for you."

Amber took the coin and gave Dale a hug and a kiss on the cheek. "Thank you for the coins, they are perfect for my collection."

"You are very welcome." Dale saw movement outside the kitchen window. "Who is that coming up your walk?"

Gail looked out the window. "Look Amber, Susie from next door is coming to play with you."

Dale and Gail talked for most of the afternoon with only the occasional interruption when Gail went to check on the girls. Dale had been more than understanding of the situation and put Gail at ease. "I know how Amanda feels about wanting her birthmother to be a part of her wedding."

"You do?"

"I may be a man, but give me credit for noticing things and having feelings."

Gail placed her hand on Dale's arm and spoke softly. "I know that you have feelings. I also know that Amanda means a great deal to you."

Dale placed his hand on Gail's hand resting on his arm and smiled. "Out of respect for Amanda's wishes to find her birthmother I haven't been pushing the issue of proposing marriage and being engaged."

Gail sat up straight, folded her arms and stared intently at Dale. "I don't know if I should hug you for being so understanding of Amanda's situation; or be disgusted at how you are trying to turn the situation in your favor because you are afraid to commit to Amanda." She leaned forward and placed her hands palm down on the table in front of him. "And you probably expect me to believe that you are only thinking of her."

Dale was surprised by Gail's outburst. "I was kidding." His demeanor became serious. "My original plans for this week included a marriage proposal to Amanda in a romantic location. It was going to be perfect."

Gail reached for the phone. "You can call her right now and propose."

Dale shook his head. "I can only imagine how a long distance proposal might go over." He smiled. "I'm hoping for a hug when I propose; not an earache from a squeal of excitement."

Gail nodded her head in agreement. "I know it seems like a big deal for Amanda to have her birthmother share her joy, on her wedding day. Deep down I wished that my birthmother could have been a part of my wedding, but look at how much of my life would have been wasted if I had waited until last year to marry Wade. I'm pretty sure that he might not have waited."

Dale blinked his eyes. "What are you trying to say?"

"I'm not trying to say anything that you don't already know. If you want Amanda to be a part of your life, in a more meaningful way, you need to quit making excuses and ask her to marry you." Gail paused. "You need to do it before she accepts a marriage proposal from someone less deserving of her love."

Dale glanced at his watch out of habit. He already knew what time it was. He also knew what Amanda should be doing right now. Dale wanted to be with Amanda; in fact he knew that he needed to be with Amanda. He wasn't aware of the tears on his face until Gail gently handed him a tissue after she had dabbed at a tear before it fell. He excused himself and went to make a phone call.

The phone rang at Amanda's apartment and was picked up on the second ring, but Amanda was not the person who answered. It was a man who answered the phone. A man whose voice Dale had never heard before. Dale recovered from the surprise and gathered his thoughts. "Is Amanda there?"

The man spoke in an abrupt manner. "Yes she is and whom shall I say is calling?"

Dale could feel a growing resentment for this man he had never met. "Tell her it's Dale."

There was a condescending tone to the voice. "And who is Dale?"

Dale was losing patience with the game. "Tell Amanda that Dale Evers wishes to speak with her."

The man slowly repeated the name a couple of times as if trying to remember something and then said, "Ah yes, Dale Evers, the man who I hear from the girls in the office is too afraid to propose to Amanda." There was a brief pause, when the man spoke again there was a sneer in his voice. "You really do need to take care of that issue before you have competition for the affections of this wonderful lady." There was another pause, this time the voice was taunting. "Too late, you do have competition – me." The man then hung up the phone leaving a confused and upset Dale listening to a dial tone.

Dale was uncertain what to think about this turn of events but one thing was certain, he was going to get to the bottom of this. He was about to hit redial but stopped. Dale decided to call back in an hour. If the man was still there Dale would have some serious questions to ask Amanda that should be asked in person and not over the phone.

If Dale had never wanted to come to Consuela's wedding before this turn of events, he most definitely didn't want to be there now. He regained control of his emotions and put on a brave face as he went to join the family. Wade was home from work, but was in the garage working on his project car. Jason was doing a raid on the kitchen pantry, and was excited to see Dale enter the kitchen to join him.

"Jason, how are things going?"

"Good." Jason said as he stuffed a piece of cake into his mouth.

Dale opened the refrigerator and removed a carton of milk. "Would you like a glass of milk with your cake?" Dale saw the brief hesitation and uncertain look from Jason and smiled. Past history and practical jokes involving food would have made him stop and consider the offer before accepting.

"Yes please." was the muffled reply as another piece of cake entered the cavity of certain doom.

Judging by the amount of cake remaining in the tray and the rate of consumption Dale took one of the larger glasses from the cupboard and filled it almost to the top. It was difficult not to laugh when the offered glass of milk was received with another brief look of uncertainty before being used to chase the remnants of cake into the bottom of a seemingly hollow leg. Dale chuckled to himself as he remembered just how much Jason could eat. He waited until the glass was empty, and was surprised that there was still some cake left when the cake tray was put away. "Would you like some more milk?"

"No thank you. I don't want to ruin my appetite for dinner. Mom is planning to make my favorite meal and I think that I owe it all to you." Jason wiped his mouth and used the camera of his cell phone to check for any crumbs that he might have missed. "So how are things with Amanda?" Jason asked as he reached into the pantry and removed a package of cookies.

Dale had reached for the handle of the refrigerator door but stopped when the box of cookies was opened. "Things are fine. Why do you ask?"

Jason chewed the cookies in his mouth until he could speak. "Have you asked Amanda to marry you?" The small cookies disappeared two at a time until there was no more room at the inn and a longing look was being cast in the direction of the empty glass.

Dale smiled as he poured some milk into the glass and watched Jason guzzle it down. "Not yet. If things had worked out this week I would have already proposed."

Jason burped as he once again wiped his mouth and checked for crumbs. "What is taking you so long? The whole world knows how you feel about Amanda."

Dale returned the milk to the refrigerator and firmly closed the door. Before the conversation went any further the sound of the special ring tone for Vicki was heard on Jason's phone. Jason got up to leave the kitchen and was almost out of earshot from Dale before he answered the call. "Hi Vicki, I'm almost ready to go. I was just talking with my uncle Dale and lost track of the time." Jason returned to the kitchen just long enough to pass on a message. "Vicki says hello."

"Hello Vicki." Responded Dale as he glanced at the clock. It had only been twenty minutes since he had tried to call Amanda but it seemed like hours as the frustration of talking to that man with Amanda started to eat him up inside. He pushed away from the kitchen table with purpose as he went to call Amanda. Several cleansing breaths were required to calm him before he dialed the number. He listened to the phone ring and hoped that Amanda would answer the phone.

"Hello?"

The sound of Amanda's voice made Dale forget all of the emotions he was dealing with but it was difficult to hear her. There was a sound in the background that made it impossible to understand a word Amanda was saying. He tried to speak with her but the noise was too loud. Suddenly the noise was gone. "Sorry about the noise but I just had a shower and if I didn't finish drying my hair it would be an uncontrollable ball of frizzy tangles."

When Amanda mentioned that she had just washed her hair, Dale breathed deep and wondered if she had used that coconut shampoo that made him want to inhale the fragrance when she was near him. He took a deep breath and imagined that he could smell her hair as she spoke. When she had finished speaking he asked. "How are you doing? Has anything exciting happened since I left, and who answered your phone when I called earlier?"

Amanda sounded surprised. "You called earlier?"

"Yes I did." Dale felt a small surge of emotion rise to the surface but kept it in check. "A man answered your phone and then hung up on me."

"A man answered?" Amanda went silent.

Dale felt as if he was going to explode as unpleasant thoughts entered his mind during the silence. Had there been something going on with Amanda and this other fellow that he had been too blind to notice? How could he have been so stupid and not blurt out his love for her after returning from the family reunion, instead of trying to plan the perfect marriage proposal? Had he been smart, there would be no other man in her life and this would not be happening. The green-eyed monster called jealousy had almost taken control when Amanda spoke again.

"That must have been Adam."

Dale spoke without thinking. "Who is Adam, and what was he doing at your place?" Dale cringed as he felt that there may have been an unintended edge to his voice that may have come across wrong. Amanda was slow to respond to the question and the longer it took her to respond, the worse he felt. Dale felt the urge to ask her forgiveness for doubting her and thinking that something was going on. He drew a breath and was about to make a fool of himself in the name of love when Amanda spoke.

"Adam is the wonderful young man who arrived at the office to cover for you while you are away. He was at my place because he was kind enough to help me carry some parcels home."

Dale had become thoughtful before he asked his next question. "How long do they think that I will be away? The wedding is set for this weekend."

"We were told that you might be away indefinitely." Amanda gave a deep sigh. "How is Consuela doing?"

Dale felt that Amanda's concern for Consuela was genuine but he couldn't help thinking that he heard some uncertainty in her voice. "Consuela is doing as well as could be hoped considering that Ramón isn't here yet."

There was a genuine concern in Amanda's' voice. "That poor girl, I'm glad that you are there for her."

Dale felt that it was time to change the subject. "So what packages did Adam help you take home?"

"What?"

Dale repeated the question. "What packages did Adam help you with?"

Amanda hesitated. "Do you really want to know?"

Dale heard a warning sound in his head. Had he stepped over the line in asking? He quickly came up with an answer he felt would be appropriate. "Only if you want to tell me what was in them."

Amanda chuckled. "Well the packages were all the clothes that I bought for our trip that never happened."

Dale was relieved to hear her answer his question. "I told you that you didn't need to buy new clothes for the trip."

"I know, and you did tell me that if I did buy some they would most likely be waiting for me when we got back."

"And did they arrive in time?"

Amanda sighed. "The clothes got here late like you said they would." She paused. "Maybe it is a good thing that our plans changed. We might have been really close to where the bomb went off."

The feelings of disappointment and gratitude returned as Dale remembered just how close to the bomb they would have been. "Yes we could have been very close to the bomb, but lucky for us we weren't." Dale wiped a tear from his eye. "I am so glad that no one was by the bench when the bomb went off."

"No kidding. That could have been bad."

Dale was finding it difficult to keep the lump from forming in his throat as he thought of how close he could have come to losing Amanda in his plan for the perfect proposal. Now he felt that he might be at risk of losing Amanda to the new man in the office who was not deserving of her. He knew that he needed to finish the call before he was overcome with emotion. He felt impressed that he should tell her that he loved her, but once again ignored the feeling when he decided that this declaration of love should be done in person. Instead of saying what was in his heart, he chose to wait for a better time; even knowing that this Adam character had voiced his intent to vie for the affections of Amanda.

Before Dale could find the words to finish the conversation Amanda spoke. "Good luck with the situation surrounding the wedding." There was a pause, "Give my love to Consuela and tell her my prayers are with them."

The lump in his throat grew as the girl of his dreams could look past her concerns and show genuine concern for Consuela and Ramón. He swallowed hard to clear his throat. "I'll tell Consuela that you are praying for Ramón's arrival and that you send your love." He took a deep breath. "As for the situation surrounding the wedding, I'll need all the luck I can get. If Ramón arrives in time to marry Consuela, some young girl won't have to take out a contract on me for her not being a bridesmaid."

The comment intrigued Amanda. "Do tell."

Dale took a deep breath. "Apparently the young girl has been told by her mother that it was my fault for her not being a flower girl when the last wedding was cancelled."

"Who is the girl's mother?"

"The girl's mother is Ramón's sister and she doesn't believe what people are saying about why the wedding was cancelled."

"So why is she upset with you?"

"It seems that her mother believes that the last wedding was cancelled because of my relationship to Consuela and the girl believes her mother. So with me being here they are worried that this wedding might be cancelled and are doing all that they can to keep us apart."

Amanda started to laugh. "Good luck and I hope that the girl gets her wish of being Consuela's bridesmaid. Let me know how the story ends."

Dale listened to the snickers and laughter a few moments. "I will tell you all about it when I return, and I know how the story ends." Dale placed the receiver on the cradle and sat back in the chair. He gave a big sigh as he rubbed his face with his hands and muttered softly. "Why do I have a problem telling Amanda that I love her? The end of the call would have been a perfect time and once again I blew it." As he turned the chair he was surprised to find that Wade had entered the room.

Wade placed some papers onto the desk. "You sir, sound like a man with girl problems."

CHAPTER FOUR

$\mathcal{R}$amón Ramirez awoke to the smell of sea air and the sounds of seagulls close by. He opened his eyes and realised that he must have fallen asleep on the beach and never made it back to his room. Ramón had a headache and was hungry. He hoped that it wasn't too late for breakfast and that today's offering was as good as the other days had been. Ramón saw a young couple walking along the beach and his thoughts turned to Consuela. Oh how he missed her. He had not lost track of time and knew that their wedding was scheduled to take place in a few days. The bachelor party was over but Ramón and his best man were still on this unknown island paradise with no idea when they would be leaving.

Ramón may have been in a tropical paradise but now he was miserable; more miserable than he had ever been in his life. Even more miserable than he had been when Consuela had sent him and the bride's maids packing on the night before their first planned wedding. Ramón returned to his room and waited for his breakfast to be delivered. He watched the door open and then watched the girl's every move as she entered his room and approached the table.

She tossed the beach towel laying on the table to the floor as she positioned the tray of food in front of the chair pushed up to the table. She then stood up straight to stretch and then adjust her revealing swimsuit. She pulled the chair away from the table before she removed the napkin from the tray and snapped it open with a flick of her wrist as she motioned for Ramón to sit up to the table. "You should eat while the food is still warm."

Ramón remained motionless. "What are you doing here?"

The girl smiled and once again motioned for him to come. "I am here to take care of your needs before you leave us to be with your beloved Consuela."

Ramón never moved. "What is on the menu this morning?"

"Anything you like. Your wish is my command." The girl said in a sultry voice as she stretched and arched her back. She waited a few moments before she lifted the cover to reveal the food and ate one of the pieces of bacon. "If the current desire of your heart is still about food let's see what we have. Today the cook has prepared for you an omelette with a side of hash brown potatoes and one piece of bacon." She wiped her mouth. "And a tall glass of orange juice."

Ramón moved towards the table.

She replaced the cover on the food and waited for Ramón to take his place at the table. Once he was seated she placed the napkin across his lap and gave his knee a playful squeeze. "Enjoy."

Ramón grabbed her hand and pulled her towards him until his nose was close to hers. "Marta you were Consuela's Maid of Honor and cost me my first chance to marry Consuela – it will not happen again." He released his grip. "Why are you and all of the other girls throwing yourselves at me? Can you not see that I am a changed man and my heart is loyal to Consuela?" Ramón held her arm a few seconds longer before he released it and pushed her away from him. "How did you become part of the bachelor party my best man planned for me? He doesn't know you."

Marta rubbed her arm where Ramón had held her and glared at him. "Without me there would have been no bachelor party that you have always dreamed of."

Ramón gave a puzzled look. "What makes you say that?"

Marta smiled. "Juan is a nice boy but is not capable of planning such an event. He couldn't even plan a trip to the washroom." She moved towards the door. "The only part of the plan Juan was responsible for was letting me know when your car was leaving the embassy so that I could have you brought here to my Uncle's private island for the party."

"Why would you do this thing?" Ramón slid the tray of food away from him and tossed the napkin onto the table as he stood.

Marta stood her ground as Ramón moved towards her. "I did it because I love you and wanted to know for sure that you do not have feelings for me and what I have to offer."

Ramón stood in front of Marta. "Have you and the other girls been tormenting me to test my loyalty to Consuela?"

Marta moved away from Ramón. "Maybe your loyalty to Consuela is not the loyalty being put to the test. I understand that Dale Evers is with Consuela as we speak."

Ramón glared at her. "That is impossible. Dale called to tell me that he had prior commitments and would be unable to attend the wedding."

Marta held her ground and glared back at Ramón. "Dale's plans changed when I was able to convince his boss that there was a situation with the wedding that only Dale could handle."

Ramón pointed to the door and indicated that it was time for Marta to leave. "Dale Evers is a good friend who cares about Consuela and her happiness. I trust him with my life."

Marta snorted. "How sweet, but can you trust him with the girl who is soon to be your wife?"

Ramón clenched his jaw. "I trust Dale and I trust Consuela's loyalty to me. When I see her next I am going to tell her what you have done."

Marta smiled. "I think not."

Ramón was curious at the confidence in the response. "What makes you so sure that I won't tell Consuela what has happened to me?"

Marta laughed a laugh that was almost sinister. "I can't think of any conversation you might have with Consuela ending well when you tell her that while you were missing – you were on an island with me."

Amanda shuffled some papers on her desk and filed them in an attempt to avoid looking in the direction of Dale's office. The office should be empty while Dale was away on assignment at Ramón and Consuela's wedding, but it wasn't. Amanda quickly glanced towards the open office door and saw Adam sitting behind the desk where Dale should be. It felt awkward when she saw Adam because there was an unexpected attraction for this well groomed and intelligent man. It definitely didn't help the situation when Amanda had random thoughts that made her blush and betrayed her devotion to Dale. At those times Amanda held to the question that helped keep her feelings towards this man in check. "Why did Adam hang up on Dale and then not tell her that Dale had called?"

One morning Amanda arrived at work to find a bouquet of flowers sitting on her desk. She pressed her nose into the bouquet and took a deep breath to enjoy the fragrance of her favorite flowers. She looked for a card in the bouquet– but found none. It wasn't normal to receive flowers from Dale without at least a card, but then again it wasn't normal for a bouquet of flowers from Dale to be this large.

Soon after Amanda had abandoned the search for a card, Adam entered the office wearing a very expensive and flattering suit that enhanced the appearance of his well developed arms and shoulders. Amanda saw him enter and quickly looked away before anyone could notice that she had been admiring the suit longer than she thought was acceptable. She wanted to take a second look but remembered the Bible story of King David and Bathsheba and how it had ended badly. Amanda resisted the urge to look because she knew that the next look would be long enough to be classified as a stare. She was able to ignore Adam by focusing on the beautiful bouquet of flowers in front of her until Adam came over to Amanda's desk to admire the flowers with her.

Adam smelled the flowers and gently touched them as he admired the arrangement. "I approve, the sender of these flowers has very good taste." Adam stepped back until he could see Amanda and the flowers at the same time. "The colors of the flowers are perfect in the way they bring out the beautiful color of your eyes." He moved the baby breath to one side and looked into the center of the stems.

Amanda moved the flowers closer to her and away from Adam. "May I help you?"

Adam pulled his hand back. "I'm sorry. Is there any mail for me today?"

Amanda checked the stack of envelopes and handed two of them to Adam. "There you go, that ivory colored envelope sure smells nice."

Adam took a whiff and looked at the return address on the envelope. "It certainly does, I'll tell my aunt that you approve of her perfume." He returned to Dale's office and removed his suit jacket to reveal a form fitting shirt that enhanced the appearance of an upper body that begged to be admired without the distraction of a shirt.

Amanda didn't know what to think about Adam's answer concerning who the sender of the aromatic letter was, but she highly doubted that the letter came from his aunt. Amanda had watched the jacket being removed and became aware that she was not the only lady in the office to notice what hook the jacket ended up on. She was surprised when Jean came up behind her. "Not your ordinary out of shape middle aged diplomat is he?"

"What?" Amanda turned to see the large smile on Jean's face. She could feel a blush coming to her own face. Her quick second glance at Adam had turned into a stare, but Amanda was quick to notice that she had not been alone in her fascination with Adam as none of the other girls were getting any work done either.

Jean chided. "That man could make me forget about my own boyfriend. Especially if he paid attention to me like he does to you."

Amanda became guarded. "Why would you say that? Adam pays just as much attention to everyone else as he does to me."

Jean smiled. "Then why are you the only one with flowers on your desk. You and I both know that they are way too nice to have come from Dale."

Amanda felt herself becoming defensive. "Why would you say that?"

Jean reached out to touch the flowers. "When was the last time Dale sent you flowers this nice at work?"

Amanda looked at the flowers she had already conceded were nicer than the usual fare from Dale and sighed. "Dale has never sent anything larger than a small forget me not bouquet."

"I rest my case." Jean returned to her desk.

Amanda was flustered and didn't know what to think. Was it possible that this gorgeous hunk of humanity in Dale's office could be interested in her? She looked at the flowers with the yet to be determined sender and slid them to the corner of the desk. Her heart belonged to Dale and until she knew differently – these flowers were from Dale.

A few days later Amanda arrived at work to find that her desk was neatly arranged and all of her papers she was unable to finish the day before were sorted and ready to be filed. She expected to see wilted flowers in the vase and was prepared to dispose of them, but instead she was surprised to find that the flowers in the vase were fresh cut that day. Amanda looked around to see who was in the office that could have done this, but only gave a small sigh when she saw that she was alone. Dale couldn't have done it because he was half a world away. Maybe Jean was right and Adam did bring the flowers, but why? Amanda wanted to know who had sent the flowers but she didn't want to make a fool of herself by asking Adam if he had sent them until she knew for sure that Dale hadn't sent them.

CHAPTER FIVE

*D*eceiving Consuela about Ramón's absence did not make Dale happy but he found that he was even less happy when he lied to himself about what he felt when he was alone with Consuela. In spite of these feelings Dale knew that he would find his happiness married to Amanda so he only went to the embassy when his presence was requested. Dale spent much of his time visiting with family and helping his parents. Dale was saddened when he realised just how many years had passed since he had spent meaningful time with his parents. It saddened him even more to know that no amount of visits now could ever make up for the time he had spent away from family. His father was moving much slower than Dale remembered him moving at the last family reunion. There were times during his visit that his father seemed confused but had been helped through those awkward moments with prompts from his wife. Both parents had heart issues, and his mother's heart issue had flared up a few months earlier to give everyone quite a scare. It had been especially hard on Dale being so far away and unable to be there for her the way he would have liked to be. Dale always knew that his parents wouldn't live forever but always thought that the day of a final farewell was still a long way off. Visiting with them this trip had made him more aware than ever that the day might be closer than he wanted to admit.

Today Dale went to visit his parents and did some chores around the house as he tended to the yard the way he had done when he still lived at home; only this time he was surprised at how glad he was to do the chores. Dale was tired at the end of the day from his labors but was glad that he had taken this time to be with his parents. When he was satisfied that things around the house and yard were in order he was ready to leave. He hugged his father who had tears in his eyes.

"Son, I am so glad that you came to visit." The embrace was sincere and tender. "I wish that you lived closer so we could spend more time together."

Dale felt a lump in his throat. "So do I dad, so do I."

His mother had a bag of his favorite homemade cookies in her hand as she extended her arms for a hug. "These cookies are for you. Don't let Jason see them or you will not have any left to enjoy."

Dale opened the bag of warm cookies and inhaled. "These are my favorites but when did you have time to make them?"

"I made them while you were helping your father with the yard." She took them from his hands and set them on the table before she wrapped her arms around Dale. "Thank you for coming, it means a lot to us."

"It means a lot to me as well." Dale knew that his eyes had only glistened and the tears had never escaped his eyes after the hug with his father, but now they were starting to flow. Dale was becoming emotional at the thought that this might very well be one of the last times he would be able to hug his parents.

His mother picked up the bag of cookies and placed it in his hand. "You enjoy these and know that we love you more than words can tell."

Dale took the bag. "Is there anything else I can do for you before I go?" He watched as both of his parents looked at the pictures of family hanging on the wall.

His mother reached out to straighten the pictures of his siblings and their families before reaching for his picture. She then turned to face Dale. "Promise me that when you return home, that you will propose to that wonderful girl we have heard so much about. Your father and I are still hopeful that we will be able to attend your wedding."

The guilt that Dale felt at that moment was immense. He now felt that he had not only disappointed Amanda by taking so long to propose, but now there was a chance that if he took much longer his parents wouldn't be able to share his joy. He swallowed hard. "I promise that I will propose to Amanda the moment I see her."

Dale drove away from his parent's house slower than usual and could see them in the rear view mirror waving until he was out of sight. His mother's parting comment stuck in his mind and he couldn't stop thinking about it. This guilt that he felt at that moment for disappointing his parents made Dale's hesitation in proposing to Amanda even more hurtful.

All of the excuses he had used over the years to justify being away from family were now haunting him. He knew that he had lost many choice opportunities to be with those he loved and will never get them back. His brother Jerry, who was his best excuse for being so far away, was now working closer to family so Dale's reason for being on the other side of the world to watch out for him no longer existed.

Dale thought of all the promotions he had applied for that would have brought him closer to family, promotions he had been deemed unqualified for by his supervisor. Dale smacked the steering wheel, the reason he had been unqualified was because his supervisor never allowed him to take the necessary training. The drive to Gail's gave Dale a chance to think and the main question he tried to answer was. *What is it that kept him doing what he did?* The enjoyment for the job had left shortly after the arrival of his supervisor. The more Dale thought about it, the only thing that made his job feel worthwhile was being with Amanda. Dale clenched the steering wheel and took several deep breaths. Because of this supervisor he was here on assignment to attend a wedding he never wanted to attend, while some stranger was making time with his girl. Dale wanted to be with Amanda but more importantly he wanted to put a ring on her finger.

Dale arrived at Gail's house as Gail and Wade were getting ready to leave with Amber. They were acting different than normal and actually seemed on edge.

Gail greeted Dale with a hug. "Thank goodness you're home."

Dale was curious to know the reason for this behavior. "What is going on?"

Wade took his car keys from the hook. "We need to go to the mall and get Jason from the mall security office." He stopped walking and turned to Dale. "I don't know how long we will be but it would sure help if you could watch Amber while we are gone."

Dale was now even more curious about what was happening. "What did Jason do?"

Gail took a deep breath. "We're not sure what is going on but we need you to watch Amber and make sure that she eats. There is plenty of food in the pantry."

Dale wanted to go to the mall and see what his nephew was into but remembered what had happened the last time he had allowed his curiosity to get the best of him. "Go rescue your son. I will take care of Amber."

Once Wade and Gail were gone Dale found Amber in the family room. "What would you like to eat?"

"I don't know."

Dale was in no mood to play games or cook so he had a plan. "Would you like me to cook a big dish of Brussels sprouts and other healthy foods or would you like to go with me for chicken strips, French fries and an ice cream sundae?"

Amber slid from her chair and grabbed her coat as she headed for the door. "Can I have a banana split instead?"

"You may have whatever you wish." Dale grabbed the car keys and they left the house.

Dale and Amber were greeted by Gail when they returned home. "Did the two of you have a good time?"

Dale helped Amber take off her coat. "We had a wonderful time and went to her favorite restaurant for chicken strips and ice cream."

Gail turned to Amber. "What kind of ice cream did you have today?"

"I had the jumbo banana split with brownies and ate it all." Amber stopped talking and raised her hand to her mouth as she burped. "I don't feel so good mommy."

Wade was passed in the hallway as Gail took Amber to the bathroom. He came to talk with Dale. "What's wrong with Amber?"

Dale sighed. "It must have been something she ate. For a moment at the restaurant I thought that I was paying to feed Jason."

Wade smiled. "Amber does have a healthy appetite at times; especially when it comes to eating chicken strips and ice cream."

"So I noticed." Dale looked towards the door to make sure that Gail wasn't near enough to hear. "The only way to keep Amber from asking a million questions about me and Amanda was to keep her busy eating so I kept buying her more ice cream."

"So how much ice cream did she eat?"

Dale coughed softly. "Two sundaes, one chocolate and one strawberry; a jumbo banana split with brownies and then I bought her a chocolate dipped cone for the drive home." Dale paused. "Please don't tell Gail what happened."

Wade winked. "Your secret is safe with me." Wade turned and started towards the kitchen.

Gail joined them in the kitchen a few minutes later. "Besides the ice cream how much did Amber eat?"

Dale never hesitated to respond. "She ate a chicken strip basket with fries and a large glass of root beer."

Gail folded her arms and sighed. "Even you should know that is way too much food for a little girl. Next time she only needs a child's portion of chicken strips and a small sundae, and definitely not a banana split."

Dale nodded to show that he understood before he asked, "So what was the excitement at the mall with Jason?"

Wade took a handful of popcorn from the bowl on the counter. "It was all a misunderstanding caused by an overzealous security person who thought that because Jason's friend was shoplifting; Jason was an accomplice."

Dale looked at Wade. "Do you think that Jason could be shoplifting?"

Wade grabbed another handful of popcorn. "The police officer who met us at the mall told me that this was not the first time the boy with Jason had been caught shoplifting and he recommended we encourage Jason to keep his distance from him to avoid further incidents."

"What did Jason have to say about that?"

Wade reached for a glass of water. "Jason has no problem with that. He told me that his reason for going to the mall with the boy was to purchase a birthday gift for Gail. It was while he was deciding what color he should choose that the security person took him to the office."

Dale's phone rang and after a brief conversation Dale excused himself. It seemed that once again his presence was required at the embassy and a car was being sent for him. He was getting tired of helping sort out other people's problems when his own problems were more pressing than theirs and needed his attention. Dale was having trouble finding a happy place in his mind as he arrived at the embassy and was escorted to the ambassador's office; most likely to find out what new lie he would have to tell Consuela.

Dale arrived at the ambassador's office where he was greeted warmly. "Dale I am so glad that you are here. I can wait no longer to reveal why Ramón has yet to arrive."

This statement brought Dale's thoughts to the present situation. "Why the sudden change of heart?" Dale watched the actions of the ambassador. "Are you not concerned about being asked by Ramón's family for updates that you don't have?"

The glance across the room at Dale wasn't as friendly as the greeting had been. "Yes, that is still a concern but at least I won't have a war break out in my embassy amongst the wedding guests."

The answer intrigued Dale. "Why would you have a war break out?"

The ambassador sat behind his desk. "My family members are reminding people why the last wedding was cancelled and are claiming that Ramón is not here because he is having one last fling; once again cheating on Consuela before they are wed."

Dale rubbed his chin. "That isn't good."

The ambassador ran his fingers through his hair from in front of the ears to the back of his head and then scratched. "Not at all and Ramón's family are defending his honor to where fights have broken out."

In spite of all that was going on to concern the ambassador, Dale couldn't help but ask. "Did anyone get kicked?"

The wrinkles across the ambassador's brow lessened and the two men shared a chuckle. "No, so far you are the only one to feel the wrath of Cecelia."

Hearing Cecelia's name Dale raised his foot and rubbed his ankle. "How may I be of service to you today?"

There was a long hesitation as the ambassador shifted in his chair before he leaned towards Dale. "I need you to explain to Consuela why I took so long to tell her what has happened to Ramón."

Dale pulled his pant leg over his ankle and lowered his foot to the floor. "Have you at least told Consuela why Ramón isn't here yet?"

There was another moment of silence followed by a big sigh. "No, I was hoping that you would tell her while I make the announcement to the rest of the guests."

Dale picked at a piece of lint he found on his jacket and drew a deep slow breath. "Why do you want me to tell your daughter something that you should have shared with her when you first found out Ramón was missing?"

The only sound to be heard in the room was the rhythmic sound of the clock on the wall. The silence was broken with the answer to Dale's question.

"I want you to do this for me because you have a way to calm Consuela when bad things happen." The ambassador placed his hands over his face and rubbed against his whiskers. "While you are speaking with Consuela, I will call the outspoken family members into my office to show them the abduction video."

Dale took another deep breath and then exhaled until he could push no more air from his lungs. He looked across the desk. "I will do this for you, but I still think that you should be the one to tell her." Before Dale could finish speaking there was a knock at the office door.

The conversation at the door was almost in a whisper that made it difficult for Dale to hear, let alone understand what was being said. The door closed and the ambassador returned to where Dale was sitting. "You are absolutely right. I should be the one to inform Consuela about Ramón." He motioned for Dale to rise. "Please join me."

Dale was reluctant to join the ambassador in delivering the message after so much time had passed without telling Consuela the truth about Ramón's absence. He joined the ambassador because he understood that Consuela might need someone to turn to for support and would be there to offer her a shoulder to cry on.

They arrived at the top of the stairway overlooking the main entry and waited for a few moments observing how the families interacted with each other, or more how they didn't interact with each other. The ambassador waited a few more seconds before getting the attention of the guests.

"My friends." He waited until there was silence in the hall. "These past few days many of you have approached me to ask if I knew anything about where Ramón and his best man are." He looked around the room and stopped to look into the eyes of each and every guest. "Ramón and Juan were detained along the way but are now about to join us. Let the wedding celebrations begin."

There was murmuring among the guests that went silent as the outside doors opened and Ramón and Juan appeared. The once menacing tone of the conversations was now upbeat and friendly as the men were welcomed with open arms. The throng of people parted when Consuela arrived and she rushed forward to greet the man of her dreams with a long overdue embrace. It was a touching scene and all eyes were on the couple. All eyes it seemed, except the eyes of one little girl and her mother who even at this moment of joy glared at Dale.

Dale leaned close to the ambassador. "Mr. Ambassador, when did you know about Ramón being in town?"

"I just found out. The knock at the door was my assistant telling me that Ramón and Juan were at the front gate preparing to walk up the driveway to the embassy."

Dale watched the joyful reunion of his friends. He was happy that Ramón was doing well and in the arms of the girl he loved. "Sir, are you ever going to tell Consuela that you knew what happened to Ramón?"

There was a playful wink. "No, to reveal that I knew what happened and to have never told anyone is not a good way to start a long term relationship with Ramón's family."

They shared a brief chuckle. "Mr. Ambassador you are a wise man." Dale shook hands with the ambassador. "I feel it will be best if I were to leave now so that the wedding preparations can begin in earnest, without me being a distraction."

"I agree. My security detail will protect your ankles from Cecelia as you leave. It would appear that once again she has you in her sights." The ambassador was slow to release his grip on Dale's hand. "Thank you for being a true friend to Consuela."

"It is a pleasure to be her friend and I will see you at the wedding."

Dale was grateful that the situation with Ramón had ended well and there was no more need to continue with any deception. All that was left for him to do now was attend what he hoped would be a wedding ceremony and reception that were memorable for all the right reasons. Seeing the look in Cecelia's eyes as he passed her made Dale wonder if Cecelia would ever stop looking at him like public enemy number one.

The excitement over the return of Ramón was affecting everyone. It surprised Dale that Eduard was more talkative than normal during the drive to Gail's house. Before they had gone very far Eduard asked a question. "Senor Evers, what do you think really happened to Ramón?"

Dale was caught off guard by the question. "Why do you ask?"

Eduard looked uncomfortable. Talking about other people's affairs was not in his comfort zone. There was a deep breath and a slow deliberate exhale. "Everyone seems to have their own idea about why Ramón was late arriving for his wedding but most of the ideas make no sense at all."

Dale sensed the discomfort and tried to put Eduard at ease. "Really, there are that many different ideas and theories?" he chuckled as he smiled at Eduard. "What do you think happened?"

"I'm not sure what I think." Eduard paused. "After what happened to make Consuela cancel the failed wedding, I tend to agree with the embassy staff members who think that Ramón and his best man went on one last fling."

This revelation took Dale by surprise. "They really think that?"

"Yes they do. They also think that if that was the case, Ramón was very inconsiderate to make Consuela sick with worry while he and his best man had a big bachelor party."

Dale could see how the staff could come to that conclusion with their loyalty to Consuela. Knowing what people were thinking would be a good thing to know should he need to defend Ramón in the court of public opinion. "What do the other people think happened?"

Eduard grinned. "Some believe Consuela when she would say that he was having flight problems that made him late."

Dale saw the grin. "Why are you smiling when you say that?"

There was a twinkle in Eduard's eyes. "That sounds like something you would say to keep her from worrying. Am I right?"

Dale was impressed with Eduard's insight. "Yes you are. How did you guess?"

Eduard had a large grin. "It sounds like the way you described your trip coming here."

Dale was glad he hadn't said anything negative to Eduard. "Fair enough, what else do people think?"

Eduard pulled the limousine onto the freeway. "Cecelia and her mother think that you had Ramón abducted so that you could marry Consuela in his absence."

"What do you think about that?" Dale asked in anticipation of the answer.

Eduard did a shoulder check. "I think that they have crazy genes and I hope for Consuela's sake that they are only with the women in Ramón's family and not with Ramón."

Dale and Eduard shared a laugh. "Why would they think that I had abducted Ramón?"

Eduard became more serious. "They remember how close you and Consuela were after the cancellation of the last wedding and Ramón was sent away with the bridesmaids." Eduard looked at Dale in the mirror. "Do you know what really happened?"

Dale considered his words carefully. "I'm not sure what happened." In the reflection from the rear-view mirror Dale could see the look in Eduard's eyes and sensed that his answer had fallen short. Dale wished he could give a better answer but he knew that he couldn't. "Eduard the only ones who can tell us what happened is Ramón and his best man, and I'm sure that we are not the only ones looking forward to knowing the truth when they decide to share the story about their adventure. Until we know for sure what happened I would keep my ideas to myself." Dale winked. "You know how gossip can make a good situation go bad."

The car turned the last corner onto the street where Gail lived and stopped in front of her house. Before Eduard could put the transmission into park Dale asked, "I'm curious, putting all these theories aside Eduard, what do you think happened?"

"This whole situation is a mystery to me."Eduard shrugged his shoulders. "I think that Ramón loves Consuela too much to hurt her again by having a party with other girls; and to make her worry about his safety." Eduard turned to Dale. "I also think that if he had been abducted, like some would like to believe, he wouldn't look as if he has been at a resort and put on some weight." Eduard exited the vehicle and opened the door for Dale as he continued speaking. "I also think that Consuela is very lucky to have a friend like you." He paused. "What happened these past few days is of no concern to anyone but Ramón and Consuela and I wish them all the best." Eduard closed the door. "I will be here at ten o'clock the day of the wedding to pick you up."

CHAPTER SIX

Dale was happy to have more time to himself now that his services were no longer required to keep the bride calm with the groom missing. He spent most of his time with Wade at work to avoid the endless questions about Consuela and Amanda from the girls in the house. Wade had always told Dale that should he ever come to his senses and move back to this part of the world there was a job waiting for him. Dale thought that this would be the perfect opportunity to experience the working life Wade was offering.

The time with Wade had given Dale a chance to have meaningful conversations, without being asked every second sentence why a ring was yet to be placed on Amanda's finger. Tomorrow was the day of the wedding that was keeping him from being with his beloved Amanda. Dale could hardly wait for the wedding to be over so that he could catch the first flight home.

They returned home and were met by Gail as they entered the house. Wade received a welcome hug and a kiss, while Dale received a hug and was handed a piece of paper with a note written on it.

"What's with the note?" Dale asked as he opened the fold to reveal the writing. He looked at the note and pursed his lips.

"Is there something wrong?" Gail looked concerned. "Who is this man who called and left the message to have you call him immediately when you returned home?" She let Wade escape her grasp and disappear down the hallway to the den. "The man seemed both annoyed and curious as to why you had left your phone behind."

Dale tucked the note into his shirt pocket. "I left the phone on the dresser in case there was a phone call related to the wedding tomorrow. I have no desire to help them keep the peace or deal with whatever else that might come up." Dale sighed as he rubbed his eyes. "I just want to go home to Amanda."

Gail smiled and started to speak.

Dale held up his hand and pointed his index finger at her. "Not a word about proposing to Amanda when I get back. I will propose when the time is right, and it will be very soon I promise."

Gail continued to smile. "I'm sure it will be. Mom phoned to tell me of your promise to her."

Amber joined them in the hallway. "Mom have you seen the coins Uncle Dale gave me?"

"I saw them when he gave them to you but never really looked at them that close. Would you like to show them to me now?"

Amber pursed her lips as she clenched her jaw. "I would show them to you if I could find them." Amber turned to Dale. "Do you have any more coins?"

Dale reached into his pocket and removed the contents of his pocket. He showed Amber two quarters, a dime, three nickels and a small ball of lint that he flicked out of his hand and then picked up off of the floor under the watchful eye of Gail. "Sorry kiddo that's all the coins I have."

Gail knelt down in front of Amber. "I will help you look for them later. They have to be here somewhere."

Amber hugged her mother and went to her bedroom to continue her search for the coins.

Gail watched Amber until she was out of sight. "That is very odd. Amber doesn't misplace things – especially money."

The conversation was interrupted by the sound of the door bell.

Gail answered the door and stepped outside to welcome her visitor with a hug. "Alex. What a pleasant surprise." Gail stepped back into the house and motioned for Alex to enter. "Please do come in."

Alex entered the house followed close behind by a young man who was holding onto the fingers of her left hand.

When the door was closed Gail began the introductions. "Dale, you remember Alex don't you?"

Dale extended his hand towards Alex. "Of course I do. I would recognize her anywhere, even without the uniform."

Alex stepped aside and motioned towards the young man standing next to her. "Dale I would like you to meet my good friend Chad Hill."

Dale greeted the young man with a firm handshake. "I am pleased to meet you Chad."

"Nice to meet you Dale, I have heard so much about you."

"You have?" Dale looked at Alex and then at Gail.

"Absolutely, you are the one who helped bring these wonderful ladies back together." Chad winked. "By the way, have you proposed to Amanda yet?"

Dale was speechless as he had to wonder if there was a soul alive that didn't know about him and Amanda, and if there was he would like to meet that person.

Alex spoke up before Dale could respond. "I am glad that you are here so that I can thank you in person for all that you have done for me." She moved forward and gave Dale a hug. "So many good things have happened because you cared enough to bring Gail back into my life. She is an angel." Alex moved away and she wiped a tear.

"Yes she is. Things wouldn't be the same without Gail." Dale noticed Gail wiping at some tears without much success. "That is why we love her so much."

Dale stepped aside when Amber pushed her way into the hallway to stand next to Gail and look at both Alex and Gail wiping tears. She then turned to Dale. "Mommy did Uncle Dale do something bad to make you and Alex cry?"

Gail leaned over and gave Amber a kiss on the forehead. "No sweetheart, he did something good."

Amber's hands came to rest on her hips. "Then why are you and Alex crying?"

Alex knelt down and hugged Amber. "These are happy tears because without Dale your mom and I may never have met again."

Amber looked from Gail to Alex and then back to Gail as she shook her head. "It must be hard being an adult. I only cry when I am sad or when I hurt myself."

Dale watched the interaction between Alex and Chad. He smiled when he saw the ring on Alex's finger. "So Alex, how long have you and Chad been friends?"

"We have been friends for quite a while. Why do you ask?"

Dale winked and glanced down at her hand as he pointed to the ring that was partially hidden from view by Chad's hand. "I'm just wondering how close a friend Chad is."

Alex held out her hand. "Close enough for me to ask Gail if she would be my Matron of Honor." The hallway was filled with squeals of excitement as Gail and Alex embraced.

Gail reached to give Chad a hug. "I would be honored to be your Matron of Honor."

Alex then knelt down in front of Amber. "Amber would you be one of my bridesmaids?"

Amber gave her own squeal of excitement and joined Gail and Alex shedding tears.

Dale smiled. "Amber I thought you only cried when you were sad?"

She gave Dale a defiant look. "I must be almost an adult."

Wade came down the hallway to join the group. "What am I missing?"

Alex held out her hand. "Chad and I are engaged!"

"Congratulations." Wade embraced the couple and then placed his arm around Gail. "Let us know how we can be of assistance with your wedding."

After a few minutes of conversation in the hallway they went to sit in the living room. As Amber moved past Dale to sit next to Gail she stopped and turned to Dale. "You see Uncle Dale, girls will say yes. If you would ask Amanda to marry you, you could be getting married too!" she paused. "Would you like me to dial her number for you?"

Amber had hit Dale with the perfect ambush. He was speechless as he reached out and rubbed the top of her head. "Thank you but I'm a big boy and I can call Amanda myself."

"Then do it so I can be a bridesmaid at your wedding too." The hands once again rested firmly on those small hips.

Wade smiled at Dale. "It sounds like you have been told. Care to use my den to make the call?"

"Don't mind if I do." Dale moved past Amber as he left the room to make his call. Once in the den and the door closed firmly behind him Dale dialed Amanda's number.

"Hello?"

Dale was shocked to once again hear the voice of the inconsiderate man who had hung up on him the last time he had answered Amanda's home phone, and now he was answering her work phone as well. He wanted to give the man a piece of his mind but summoned all the restraint that he possessed. "May I please speak with Amanda?"

"And whom shall I say is calling, and what is the purpose of your call?"

Any humor that may have been with the situation was lost on Dale. "This is Dale Evers and I wish to speak with Amanda right now!"

There was a brief silence. "I'm sorry Mr. Evers but Amanda is in a meeting that will most likely last the rest of the day. I shall tell her you called?"

"Please do, and make sure that she gets the message this time."

The conversation ended when the man hung up on him. Dale was not gentle as he returned the receiver to the cradle and left the den. He passed Amber in the hallway who asked, "Did she say yes?"

He took a deep breath to compose himself before he answered his niece. She did not deserve to be the recipient of his venting. "Amanda was in a meeting so I couldn't talk to her right now."

"But you are going to talk to her."

Dale looked at the angelic face. "Yes, I am going to talk to Amanda. Now you go help your mom in the kitchen." As Amber went to the kitchen Dale went to his room to pack his bags.

As the socks and underwear landed in the suitcase his phone rang. Dale muttered as he reached for the phone. "Maybe the jerk does know what is best for him and gave Amanda the message." Dale looked at the display and dropped his head. The number was not Amanda's. He recognized it as the number from the note Gail had handed him.

"Hello?"

"Dale I am so glad to catch you before things got hectic with the wedding tomorrow. We all wish to congratulate you for how well you have handled the situation with the missing groom. Everyone is very impressed."

"Thank you sir, I'm glad that I was able to help." Dale was surprised to hear praises coming from his supervisor. He was even more surprised by what came next.

"The training courses that you have been requesting are long overdue and we want you to complete them before you return. You are scheduled to be in the next available class."

Dale could scarcely believe that he was hearing the words he had hoped to hear years earlier. "When does the class begin?"

"The class begins on the Monday following the wedding so you will be staying there a few days longer before you come home."

Dale was torn and didn't know what to think. He wanted and needed this training to qualify for the advancement he desired, but right now he had this overwhelming desire to be with Amanda so he could deal with this mystery man who kept hanging up on him. He visualized how he might deal with the man and concluded that the actions he had fantasized would not be a good career move. He took a long slow breath. "I will be there." Dale hung up and tossed the phone onto the dresser as he started to unpack.

Gail walked past the door of the room and stopped when Dale's socks landed in the dresser drawer like a football being spiked after a touchdown, and then bounce out of the drawer and onto the floor. "Is everything alright?"

Dale slumped onto the edge of the bed and put his head in his hands. "Everything is just fine."

"You don't look as if everything is fine. What's bothering you?" Gail moved the suitcase and sat beside Dale as she placed her arm around his shoulders. She had never seen Dale this emotional. "How is Amanda doing?"

"She is doing well."

"Then what is bothering you?"

Dale took a deep breath. "There is a new man in the office to cover for me. When I call to speak with Amanda he sometimes answers the phone, and then hangs up without telling Amanda that I am on the phone or that I even called."

"He must have a reason for acting this way."

Dale punched the pillow and put it into a headlock and twisted. "He does, he informed me during the first phone call that he is competing for Amanda's affections."

Gail watched Dale release his frustrations on the pillow. "Once Consuela and Ramón have finished their vows you should catch the first plane out of here."

"That was my intent until I got the last phone call from my supervisor. He is the man who left you the message."

"What did he want that has you in such a state?" Gail reached to place her hand on his.

Dale returned the pillow onto the bed and lightly brushed his hand across it as if to smooth out the wrinkles. "He wanted to congratulate me on doing a fine job with the wedding while Ramón was missing and to inform me that I can't leave just yet because I am scheduled for training on Monday and have to stay another week."

"What training is that?"

Dale wrung his hands. "The training I have been asking to receive for a very long time."

"That sounds like wonderful news." She paused. "What is so upsetting about this news?"

Dale pounded the bed with his fist. "That means I will be here for another week while that man is spending time making moves on Amanda."

Gail placed her hand on Dale's knee. "You need to send her some flowers. They say that it's the next best thing to being there."

Dale raised an eyebrow as he looked at Gail with a look of disbelief. "Seriously, that lame advertising catch phrase is the best you can come up with?"

Before Gail could respond, Amber came rushing into the room."The man with the limousine is here for Uncle Dale."

Dale looked at Amber. "Are you telling me the truth or is this something Jason asked you to say?"

Amber stepped back and looked to her mother. "The man is at the front door."

Gail motioned for Amber to come close and gave her a hug. "Thank you for telling us Eduard is here. Uncle Dale has a lot on his mind so while he goes with Eduard you can help me send some flowers to Amanda for him."

Amber squealed with delight. "O goody!"

Dale reached for his wallet but stopped when Gail raised her hand. "The flowers will be my treat; in your condition you might send the entire store inventory in one bouquet." She took Amber by the hand. "You can help me decide what the card should say."

Dale arrived at the embassy and was escorted to Consuela's room. Along the way he wasn't surprised that Cecelia seemed to appear out of nowhere and watched his every move. He stopped outside the door and listened for sounds of crying. It was silent. He looked to see Cecelia staring at him as he knocked with his special knock. "Consuela I'm here."

The door opened a crack and Consuela motioned for him to enter. Dale never made a move towards the door. "Is there somewhere more public where we can talk so Cecelia can see that nothing is going on between us?" Dale motioned towards the girl in the shadows.

Consuela looked at Cecelia. "Is there anyone in the parlour?"

"I don't know?" Cecelia said without making a move.

Consuela was gracious towards the girl. "Could you please go check? While you are gone Dale and I will stand right here and talk."

Cecelia kept her eyes on the two of them as long as she could while she walked towards the parlour.

Consuela watched until Cecelia was out of sight. "Thank you for coming on such short notice."

Dale took Consuela by the hand and clasped it in his hands. "It's my pleasure." He looked around the nearly vacant building. "Where is Ramón?"

Consuela pulled her hand from Dale's hands as Cecelia came into view. "The men are having a bachelor party in town."

Dale paused a moment. "Is that wise considering what happened before the last wedding?"

She smiled. "Nothing will happen this time I can assure you."

"How can you be so sure?"

Consuela gave a small chuckle. "My father and some of the male staff members are with them."

Cecelia returned to report that the parlour was available and then stepped back and watched the two of them intently. Consuela and Dale went to the parlour followed by their young chaperone. When they arrived at the parlour they sat in separate chairs in front of the fireplace, in clear view of the door but far enough away that their conversation would not be heard by the ever vigilant Cecelia.

Dale was curious about the reason for the meeting and leaned close to Consuela. "So why have you sent for me?"

Tears welled up in her eyes but never escaped. "I have something important to talk to you about." Consuela seemed upset as she bit her lower lip. "Ramón refuses to talk with me about what happened to him during the days before he arrived and it concerns me."

"Why does it concern you so much? He is here safe and sound."

"It concerns me because he doesn't wish to talk about it. We have promised to not keep secrets when we are married yet he refuses to confide in me now."

Dale took a moment to collect his thoughts before he responded. "Ramón knows how special you are. I doubt that he would have done anything to disappoint you and risk losing you."

"Do you really believe that?"

"I believe that with all my heart." Dale looked deep into her eyes. "Ramón loves you."

Their eyes remained locked and Dale could see the concern in her eyes as she sat silent a few moments before finally speaking. "Thank you for your insight. It gives me more to think about." They visited a while longer until the grandfather clock chimed. Consuela looked at the clock. "I'll have Eduard take you home so he can go pick up the partiers and have them home at a decent time. I look forward to seeing you tomorrow."

Dale glanced towards the door where Cecelia stood with folded arms watching them. "If for any reason the wedding does not happen. Please tell Cecelia that it wasn't my fault."

Consuela looked towards Cecelia and smiled. "Cecelia, would you escort us to the front door?"

Cecelia immediately took her place between Dale and Consuela as they walked. Whenever she saw Dale closer than she thought was appropriate her eyes looked down to his ankles causing Dale to move away.

During the ride home Dale was preoccupied with thoughts concerning Ramón and what might have happened from the time he was abducted until he arrived at the embassy. When he entered the house he was greeted by Gail. "Is everything okay with Consuela and Ramón?"

Dale smiled. "I'll say yes, but if Eduard isn't here to pick me up tomorrow and an intense looking little girl shows up here with her mother, then I am wrong."

"That sounds ominous, care to share?"

"Not really, anything I say would just be unfounded gossip so I'll keep it to myself."

Gail handed Dale a picture. "This is a picture of the bouquet we sent to Amanda."

He looked at the picture and gave a soft whistle. "I'd propose to me with a bouquet like that. Thank you sis." He gave her a hug. "What did the card say?"

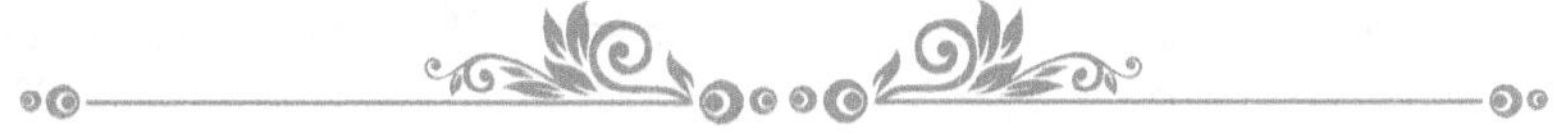

CHAPTER SEVEN

$\mathcal{A}$manda was glad that today was the day of Consuela and Ramón's wedding and that Dale would soon be on his way back to her. Amanda had been feeling nauseous and was up most of the night in the bathroom and had considered calling in sick except that she had to finish her report. She slept through her alarm and had to hurry to avoid being late. She never had time for a shower and her hair was a tangled mess that defied every attempt to tame it. Her curling iron died when she was halfway done trying to make it look presentable so she had to wet it down to make it manageable. That seemed to be working until the blow dryer quit, leaving her with the worst bad hair day she had seen in a long time. It was bad enough that she debated whether to call in sick, but duty won out over vanity and Amanda put a scarf over her head and went to work.

The impressive bouquet on her desk made Amanda feel better for her decision to come in to work, but the scarf stayed on her head. She looked in the bouquet for the card and was disappointed when none was to be found. Adam came over to her desk to talk with her and Amanda was flustered. His shirt looked tighter than any of the others he had worn to work and it looked good, while the scarf on her head was hiding the worst bad hair day ever.

Adam bent over to smell the flowers. "Who sent these flowers I wonder?"

Amanda rummaged through the flowers. "I don't know. There is no card that I can find."

"Another bouquet of flowers sent with no card – who is this inconsiderate oaf?" Adam took another whiff. "Maybe they are from Dale and he is afraid to own up to them."

Amanda pulled the flowers closer to her and glared at Adam.

Adam seemed to be enjoying the moment in spite of the look she gave him. "Or maybe you have a secret admirer who is reaching out to you."

Amanda looked away and began to sort through the papers on her desk. "Me have a secret admirer, don't be absurd." Amanda scoffed. "No one knows that I even exist, let alone where I am."

Adam smiled. "I know a lot of men who know that you exist and where you are. They only keep their distance because they know how you feel about Dale."

Amanda rolled her eyes as she looked at Adam. "You honestly think that?"

Adam placed his right hand over his heart. "I speak the truth."

Amanda smelled the flowers. "Then why did they start sending flowers now?"

Adam placed his hand on hers. "Maybe they are tired of waiting and wish to see if they can become a more meaningful part of your life."

Amanda's gaze caught his and she could feel a blush rising to her face. She looked away and began processing a stack of papers. "Until I know differently these flowers are from Dale."

When she returned home that night Amanda was emotional and near tears. She had received more flowers from an unknown sender. Hopefully they were from Dale, but maybe they were from a suitor who was willing to come forth and challenge Dale for her affections. She sat down and picked up her new book intending to read it to take her mind off of the day, but simply stared off in the distance for the longest time without ever opening the cover. After a light meal she sat down at her desk, opened her journal to the page marked by the ribbon bookmark and began to write.

Today may very well have been one of the worst days of my life. This has been more than just a bad hair day — this has been the worst day ever. I came to the realization that I may have wasted the best years of my life waiting for a man who may never propose. I fear that I have feelings for Adam and I am unable to explain why I might be attracted to him.

She sat in silence thinking before she continued writing. The tears on her fingers from wiping her eyes made it difficult to properly grasp the pen. She dried her hands.

Maybe I do need to explore my options before I am too old to catch the eye of an eligible man. I may have to accept this reality but I will remain exclusive to Dale until after my birthday. At nine o'clock the evening of my birthday if Dale has failed to propose, I will become a free agent and test the market. If he hasn't proposed by his birthday I will know it is time to move on. Maybe I have been betting on a horse that will never finish the race. As much as I hate to admit it, maybe Adam is right and there are other potential suitors out there for me who are now just testing the waters. Maybe I need to consider moving on, and maybe I need to consider Adam because of what I feel when near him. I just don't know what to think.

Amanda shed more tears as she put down her pen and replaced the ribbon bookmark in her journal before she closed it. She looked to the sky and said a small prayer. "If being with Dale is meant to be, let Dale show his love for me and propose before I make a terrible mistake. Otherwise help me find the man I am meant to be with. Amen."

CHAPTER EIGHT

When Eduard pulled the limousine in front of the Rollin's house at the appointed hour Dale gave a sigh of relief. Dale climbed into the limousine and sat back as he enjoyed the conversation with Eduard. Both men were excited at the prospects of life returning to some degree of normal. In a couple of hours if all goes well, Consuela and Ramón will be married, and maybe, just maybe, Cecelia can start to think of him as a nice man, and not public enemy number one.

Dale watched the scenery from the window as they drove to the embassy. He interrupted a brief silence during their conversation with a question. "Have you ever noticed that at every wedding there seems to be at least one guest that stands out from the rest, and usually for all the wrong reasons?"

Eduard had a puzzled look as he glanced at Dale in the rear view mirror. "Whatever do you mean Senor Evers?"

Dale saw the expression and tried to explain himself more clearly. "I am afraid that because of how Cecelia and her mother act towards me something will happen, and people will remember today because of me being a distraction and not that a wonderful couple were married."

Eduard smiled. "You worry too much. Those of us who know what you have done for Consuela will always remember you for being her friend."

Dale sat back in the seat. "You're right. I should stop worrying about nothing. Thank you."

"You are welcome." Eduard took the exit ramp off of the freeway and turned towards the embassy without saying another word.

When they arrived at the embassy Dale was escorted to the garden seating area with the other guests. Dale had hoped for an inconspicuous seat on the back row and was surprised to find his assigned seat was in the family section. He later found out that both Ramón and Consuela had wanted their dear friend, who they considered to be family, sitting with one of their families and had settled the seating debate with a coin toss. Dale considered that he had lost the coin toss when his seat was on the front row with Ramón's family; right beside Ramón's sister, mother of Cecelia. Dale delayed taking his seat until the last possible moment before he took his place beside Ramón's sister.

The groom and his groomsmen took their places. Ramón looked stunning in his robin egg blue tuxedo with a ruffle shirt. Dale had to smile when he saw how tight the shirt collar was around his neck and how tight the cummerbund appeared to be around the waist. Ramón had put on a few pounds since Dale had last seen him. The groomsmen were a sober looking bunch and at times were hard pressed to smile. Dale could only imagine that after last night's party they had been anything but sober.

When the bridal march began to play the attendees rose to their feet as they waited for the bride to make her entrance. Dale saw the pleasure in Ramón's eyes as he looked to where Consuela would enter with an unmistakable anticipation of seeing the love of his life come into view for the last time as a single woman. In this moment of joy for Ramón, Dale felt a twinge of sadness that he wasn't with Amanda, and that this wasn't their wedding day.

Two young flower girls made their way down the aisle dropping rose petals in front of the procession. Consuela and her father came into view much to the delight of all in attendance. Consuela was more beautiful than ever and her countenance glowed behind the sheer veil that couldn't conceal the smile of a happy and content young woman. The proud father escorting his daughter down the aisle beamed with pride as he walked beside her.

When the music stopped, family and friends were invited to be seated. All eyes were on the lovely couple except for those belonging to Cecelia and her mother – they were watching Dale. When the priest asked if there were any who had a reason why this couple should not be wed or forever hold your peace – Dale felt as if all eyes had turned to him. The vows were exchanged and when the time came for Ramón to kiss the bride he lovingly lifted the veil and sealed the deal.

When the couple faced their guests and were presented as husband and wife Dale gave a sigh of relief. Dale hoped that with the deed being done that the hostilities towards him were over and Cecelia would relax, but this was not the case. Cecelia and her mother became his shadow and blocked his every attempt to move towards the couple. Dale really wanted to congratulate the couple but gave up trying and figured that he would bide his time until the reception.

Dale had figured that the day might go like this and he had felt that he should be prepared for whatever might happen. He never planned on being a distraction to the festivities but it seemed that he was a distraction, in spite of being on his best behavior. He also never thought that he would be so popular with Ramón's family when they all took turns sitting with him, even though most of them never spoke a word of English.

The wedding photos of the couple and the wedding party were finally finished and the crowds around Ramón and Consuela had thinned to where he might have been able to visit but Dale kept his distance. He figured that the best time to congratulate his friends was during the receiving line at the reception and he would wait until then.

As he entered the hall for the reception Dale looked at the chart for the assigned seating. By this time he had hoped that maybe there was a table for one next to the kitchen where they wanted him to sit in seclusion, away from family. He must have lost a second coin toss as once again he found himself assigned to be in the company of Ramón's sister at their table. Before taking their seats people were invited to greet the couple in the receiving line. Not being in a hurry to find his assigned seat Dale waited until later before he took his place at the end of the line. It seemed to take forever for the line to advance to where he could even see the couple let alone speak with them. The receiving line must have been where family members from both sides felt that this was a time to catch up on old times and share a tear.

Dale was near the end of the line when he finally reached the wedding party and was standing in front of Ramón. "Congratulations my friend, you are a lucky man."

Ramón firmly grasped Dale's hand. "Thank you my friend," his gaze was fixed on Dale. "Without you being the honorable man that you are, this moment would not have been possible."

Dale was puzzled by the comment. How had he made all of this possible? He had just been a friend. "I'm just happy I could be here to share your joy."

Ramón pulled Dale close and spoke softly in his ear. "Thank you for being a true friend. One day we will have time to talk, but for now be careful." he paused, "And please, if you haven't already done so, propose to Amanda. You deserve to be as happy as we are now."

Dale wanted to ask why he should be careful but never had the chance as a rather large lady pushed him aside and began to plant kisses on Ramón's face. Now he found himself standing in front of the lovely Consuela. He was glad that she had come to terms with her concerns of the night before because she looked radiant, and he was certain that the runs in her makeup were from many tears of joy. "Congratulations Consuela, I have never seen you look so happy."

"I am happy and I thank you for being such a good friend to help me be with Ramón." Consuela reached out to take Dale's hand and then pulled Dale close for a hug and to kiss his cheek.

Dale was surprised by the kiss but enjoyed the moment. Right up until he felt a solid kick against his shin followed by a young girl screaming in pain. Cecelia had objected to Dale hugging Consuela and kicked him. Only this time it was her foot that got hurt.

A crowd gathered around Cecelia and Dale saw how people looked at him as if it was his fault. The mob was looking angry as he leaned in to speak to Consuela. "It has been a lovely day but I am leaving before anything else happens. Good bye and I wish you all the best."

Dale reached back to shake Ramón's hand and made his way from the hall. Eduard was near the door with the keys in hand and in no time Dale was on his way back to Gail's.

"What happened to Cecelia?" Eduard asked as they pulled through the gates.

Dale removed the shin pads and held them for Eduard to see. "I came prepared."

The two men shared a laugh. "It has been a pleasure Senor Evers. I hope that someday we will meet again."

"I hope so too Eduard. Enjoy the rest of the celebration." Dale stepped out of the car and waited until Eduard was out of sight before turning to the house. As he walked along the walkway he was bothered by Ramón's comment to be careful. Had Ramón meant for him to be careful because of Cecelia or was there something else? His thoughts were interrupted when he was greeted by Gail and Amber wanting to know the details of the wedding.

The following week seemed to last forever as Dale endured the training he had wanted for so long, and now that he was receiving it he was miserable as he could only think about Amanda. One day after returning to Gail's he was in the kitchen talking to her over a glass of milk and cookies when Amber came home from playing with Susie and she was noticeably upset.

"What is wrong sweetheart?" Gail asked when Amber came into the kitchen.

Amber folded her arms and put on a pouty face. "I'm mad at Susie's mom."

Dale looked at this small person with attitude and smiled. "What did she do to upset you?"

Amber pursed her lips and contorted her face before answering. "She told me to go home and mind my own business."

Both Dale and Gail found it difficult to keep from smiling.

Gail turned to the cupboard for a glass as she tried to hide her smile. "Would you like some milk and cookies?"

"Yes please." Amber climbed onto a chair. "Why would she tell me to mind my own business?"

Dale could see Gail having difficulty keeping a straight face. "So Amber, what did you ask Susie's mom that made her tell you to mind your own business?"

"I asked her why she never fixed the sticker on the back window of her van."

Dale was intrigued. "What sticker would that be?"

Amber reached for a cookie but never got it to her mouth. "The stick figures on the back window of the van showing Susie's family; one of her dad's legs is missing and needs to be fixed."

It was difficult but Dale kept a straight face as he toyed with her. "Oh my, that is serious."

Amber took a bite of cookie. "It is serious and you should go talk to her about it."

A glass of milk was placed on the table and Gail brushed the hair from Amber's eyes. "Uncle Dale is a busy man. I will talk to Susie's mom about it when I see her next okay."

"Okay." Amber finished her milk and cookies then climbed down from the chair and left the kitchen, almost bumping into Jason on her way out of the kitchen.

"Did you save any cookies for me?" Jason asked as he reached for a glass and poured some milk.

Gail slid the plate towards Jason. "There are more cookies in the oven but you need to promise me that you will save some for your father. For some strange reason he never got any of the last batch I baked."

Jason finished the cookies on the plate and downed the glass of milk as he looked at Gail. "Vicki is excited that you will be in Alex's wedding with her."

Amber came back into the kitchen. "I'm going to be a bridesmaid."

Jason put his glass in the sink. "So I hear. That sounds like it will be a good time. I wonder what kind of food they are going to serve at the reception." Jason turned to leave the kitchen then stopped. He returned to stand in front of Gail. "Did you do any cleaning in my room lately?"

Gail was curious about this question. "Why do you ask? I wouldn't dare do any cleaning without your permission. Not after the last time."

Jason seemed hesitant to say why he had asked but eventually did. "I had a box of candies in my room that have gone missing and I wondered if you knew anything about them."

"There is so much candy in your room that I am surprised you could tell if some was missing." Gail smiled at Jason. "Are you sure that you didn't eat them and just forgot that you had enjoyed them?"

Jason was firm in his response. "I know for a fact that I never ate them."

Dale chided. "You ate them. You just don't remember."

Jason shook his head. "I would remember eating these candies. I bought them special for you after you arrived."

"You bought me candy?" Dale sounded surprised and then looked intently at Jason. "What's wrong with them?"

Gail punched Dale lightly on the shoulder. "Do you always have to think the worst? Did you ever think that he bought them because he loves you?"

Dale looked at Jason. "Did you buy them because you love me?"

There was a twinkle in Jason's eye. "Not at all, a friend made me some spicy chocolate covered candies with attitude and I wanted to get your opinion."

Dale licked his lips. "Just how spicy are these chocolate covered candies supposed to be?"

Jason shrugged his shoulders. "I haven't tried them yet but I'm certain that they aren't as hot as the peppers you tricked me into eating at the family reunion last Christmas."

Dale smiled. "Not as hot? Or are they hotter?"

Gail interrupted the conversation. "Jason, maybe if you cleaned your room you might be able to find the missing candies easier."

"Perhaps but I'm not that desperate yet. Besides things have a way of showing up given enough time" Jason left the kitchen and went to his room.

They watched Jason leave and then Gail looked at Amber as she pointed to the glass Amber had left on the table.

Amber looked at the glass and then placed it in the dishwasher before she followed Jason from the kitchen.

Dale waited until Amber was out of the kitchen and he was alone with Gail. "So is there a story behind your neighbor's window sticker?"

The timer sounded and Gail took the last batch of cookies from the oven. "Yes there is but it is hard to explain to Amber."

"What is so hard to explain about a sticker?"

Gail put the cookies on the parchment paper on the counter to cool. "Amber doesn't know that the neighbors are getting a divorce and the disappearing father sticker is Tammy's way of showing how things are going."

Dale raised an eyebrow. "There is enough interest about their affairs to even care?"

"Tammy seems to think that there is." Gail placed the cookie sheet into the sink.

"Do you know what happened to cause the divorce?"A soft whistle escapes Dale's lips as he heard the details. "She doesn't sound bitter at all."

Gail finished her story. "I think that more than anything she is bitter that he has hidden all of his assets. Him, I think she is glad to be rid of."

CHAPTER NINE

Tammy Yule looked at her reflection in the full length mirror hanging behind her bedroom door. She carefully adjusted the crown until it rested squarely on her head before grasping the scepter to complete her costume. Tammy admired her reflection and had to admit that she made a stunning Queen of Hearts.

She raised the scepter and then pretended to point it at an imaginary subject as she said in a loud voice. "OFF WITH HIS HEAD!!!" just the way the Queen of Hearts had said it in Alice in Wonderland. She repeated the sequence several more times until she felt that the desired effect had been attained. Tammy was ready to announce to the world that the divorce was finalized by removing the last remnant of the husband sticker on her van window, as she declared those liberating words. "OFF WITH HIS HEAD!!!" Now all she had to do was wait for the right moment.

The side door of the house slammed shut and the sound of feet was heard on the stairs. "Mommy I'm home."

Tammy stepped into the hallway to greet Suzie. "Did you have fun playing with Amber?"

"Yes I did." Suzie reached her hand into the backpack and pulled out two shiny coins. "Look at the neat coins Amber gave me for my collection."

Tammy looked at the coins in Suzie's hand. "These are nicer than the last ones Amber gave you. She must like you a lot."

"She does."

"I'm glad that the two of you are such good friends. Put your backpack away while I get changed and then we will have something to eat." Tammy stepped back into her room and made one final flourish with the scepter before she set it down. Before she could remove the crown from her head there was a loud scream from Suzie's room. She rushed in to find her daughter in tears grasping at her throat with both hands as she struggled to breathe. Suzie's face was red and she was foaming at the mouth. Tammy grabbed the phone and dialed 9-1-1.

"This is 9-1-1. What is your emergency?"

"My daughter is turning red, foaming at the mouth and gasping for air. I think she is dying."

The door bell rang and Gail was surprised to find two serious looking police officers at her door. "Is there something wrong officer?"

The closest officer spoke. "I'm Officer Holden and this is Officer Tucker. We need to speak with Jason Rollins. Is he here?"

Gail stepped back from the door. "Yes he is. I will get him for you." Gail went into the garage where Jason was helping Wade with the project car. "Jason, two police officers are here to see you. What did you do?"

Jason had a puzzled look on his face. "I didn't do anything."

"Then why would police officers come here asking for you?"

Wade stood up from under the hood and wiped his hands. "Maybe we should go find out before you ground Jason for life." Wade led the way to the door and invited the officers into the house. "I'm Wade Rollins and Jason is my son. How may we be of service to you?"

"We need to ask Jason a few questions. Your neighbor wants him charged for assaulting her daughter Suzie."

Gail stared at Jason in disbelief. "Jason did what?"

Jason raised his hands in front of him as if to protect himself from his mother. "I never touched Suzie."

Officer Tucker spoke. "Right now we want to find out what happened to cause the pain Suzie is suffering. Pain that she claims is your fault."

Jason had a concerned look. "What did she say that I did?"

Officer Holden removed an evidence bag from his pocket. "Suzie claims that you gave her this candy that almost killed her."

Gail watched Jason's jaw drop as he looked at the bag in Officer Holden's hand. "Jason is that the box of candies that went missing from your room?"

Jason sighed. "Yes those are the Super Hot candies I had made to play a joke on Uncle Dale." He looked at Officer Holden. "Is Suzie okay?"

"She will be fine." A smile started to form on Officer Holden's face. "Maybe this will teach Suzie that crime doesn't pay."

Amber had entered the room and listened to what had happened. She came and stood beside Gail. "Mommy, do you think that Suzie took my missing coins?"

Gail put her arm around Amber. "We still don't know if they are missing."

"Yes we do. I have looked everywhere for them and they are missing." Amber placed her hands on her hips. "Have the policeman ask her if she took them. She took Jason's candy."

Gail kissed Amber's forehead. "The policemen are busy. I will talk to her mother about the coins later."

Officer Tucker smiled at Amber. "I will ask about your coins when we tell Mrs. Yule that Jason is not going to be charged with assault." He then looked at Gail. "Does your neighbor always dress up like the Queen of Hearts?"

The officers returned to the Yule residence and rang the doorbell. Tammy Yule was still in costume when she answered the door. "Are you going to arrest Jason for what he did to my Suzie?"

"No we are not going to arrest Jason."

Tammy glared at the officers. "And why not? He needs to be punished for what he did to Suzie."

Officer Holden was firm when he responded. "The Rollins family claim that items have been going missing from their home and suspect that Suzie is the cause." He waited for Tammy to calm down before he continued. "It would seem that this unfortunate situation for Suzie was brought on by her own actions. If she had left the candy in Jason's room she still wouldn't know how it tastes or how spicy it is. You may also want to speak to Suzie about some missing coins from Amber's collection."

CHAPTER TEN

*W*ade, Jason and Dale were installing the engine into Wade's project car when Dale's phone rang. As Dale listened to the caller his demeanor changed. Dale was visibly upset as he placed the phone in his pocket and smacked a fist into an open hand. "I can't believe this."

"Can't believe what?"

Dale took several deep breaths to calm his emotions. "All I want to do is to return home and propose to Amanda on her birthday. Why is that proving to be so difficult?"

"What happened now?" Wade asked as a look of frustration distorted Dale's features.

"I have just been given a training assignment to prepare me for a promotion, but this assignment will keep me from seeing Amanda. I will miss being there for her birthday." Dale was in a foul mood when he left the garage and went to the den. He sat in silence several minutes before reaching for the phone. Was his delay to place the call from not wanting to disappoint Amanda with the news or was he afraid that once again this mystery man who was vying for Amanda's affections might answer.

The phone was answered on the second ring and Dale was relieved to hear Amanda's voice. "Hello?"

The sound of her voice brought peace to his being and he wished that he was with her. "Hi Amanda it's me, Dale."

There was excitement in Amanda's voice. "Are you going to be home in time for my birthday?"

Dale's feeling of euphoria vanished. "I'll try but it doesn't look very promising. They have given me a training assignment, but if there is even the remotest chance to be there; I will be there."

There was silence before Amanda spoke again and the excitement was gone from her voice. "We can always celebrate my birthday when you get back."

Dale felt bad that for the first time in years they wouldn't be together on her birthday. "It's a date. Promise me that you won't sit alone in your apartment on your birthday. Go out with the girls and celebrate."

Amanda gave a sigh. "I promise, I will do something special to celebrate my birthday but it won't be the same without you."

Dale spoke with Amanda a while longer before ending the call.

After he had hung up Dale was determined to find a way to be with Amanda on her birthday. He devised a plan that, if everything worked to perfection would give him a chance to be with Amanda to celebrate her birthday; and still be able to make his next assignment on time. He knew that making the detour to see Amanda would cost him a fair bit of money but it was going to be worth the price. Dale worked late into the night checking flights until he was satisfied that the detour could work then rebooked his ticket for the earlier departure. His plan was to purchase the extra connecting flights for the detour along the way-just in case he encountered delays with his original flights and had to adapt. The schedule would be tight and his best chance for success was to make the first available flight after his training class to ensure that he had enough time to make it happen.

The following day Dale arrived early for the class and approached the trainer about the chances of accelerating the training so that they could be finished early on the last day. At first the trainer was reluctant to entertain the idea of being done early but must have been a romantic person at heart. After hearing Dale's plan he agreed to do what he could, but the trainer was firm in his position that the best he might be able to do was two hours if there were very few questions.

Dale was excited at the prospects of getting done early and felt a sense of relief. Until now most of the class had been content to simply take up space and breathe the air. It was doubtful that a lot of questions would be asked.

The last day of training was soon going to be over and Dale would be on his way back to Amanda. The anticipated conclusion of the class was later than the three o'clock Dale had been hoping for as for some unknown reason the class had more questions than anticipated. The delay frustrated Dale but they were still done earlier than scheduled, just not as early as Dale had hoped for. He left the classroom and raced out of the building to hail a cab. He had to hurry if he wanted his plan to work.

Dale was on edge and noticeably upset when he returned to Gail's for his bags. He had to wonder what the odds were that he would get the same driver who took the scenic route from the airport to Gail's when he first arrived; and now the man had just tried to take the long way back to Gail's. The cab pulled in front of Gail's house and Dale was not very diplomatic when he told the driver to wait for him while he went into the house for his bags. On the way to his room for to get his luggage Dale walked past the open door to Jason's room where Jason was playing a game on the computer.

Jason looked up from his game. "Uncle Dale, when do you leave?"

Dale stopped and returned to the doorway of Jason's room. "I'm on my way to the airport once I grab my bags. Why?"

Jason took a small neatly wrapped package from his dresser and handed it to Dale. "I'm glad that I was able to catch you before you left."

Dale took the package. "What's this?"

"It's a gift for Amanda from Vicki and me."

Dale was curious as to why Jason and Vicki would buy Amanda a gift. "What's the occasion?"

Jason looked at Dale with a smirk. "As if you don't know, it's her birthday and we wanted to get her something in case you forgot to."

"That is very thoughtful of you. I'll make sure that she gets it." Dale winked and left to get his bags. He slid the gift into his carryon bag and rushed from the room.

Gail was waiting for Dale at the front door with a bag of his favorite homemade cookies for the trip and to wish him well. They stepped out of the house and Dale stopped in his tracks; there was no cab waiting for him. "Where is my cab? Why would the driver leave before I paid him?"

Just as panic was about to set in Wade pulled his car to the curb in front of the house and got out of the car to join them after he had opened the trunk. "I hope you don't mind but I noticed how unhappy you were with the cab driver so I paid him and sent him on his way." Wade took one of the bags and placed it in the trunk of his car. "I hope you won't mind if I drive you to the airport. I promise to take the most direct route."

Dale was relieved that he wouldn't have any further dealings with that cab driver. "I accept your offer of a ride to the airport."

Dale was about to open the passenger door and climb into the car when he saw Amber coming towards him from Suzie's house and could see that she was upset. "Is that unhappy look on your face because you are sad to see me leaving?"

Amber stood beside Gail. "No."

Dale tried to elicit a smile. "Then what has your smile hiding on such a beautiful day."

Amber was silent a moment before she answered. "Suzie's mom told me to mind my own business and sent me home."

Gail placed her hands on Amber's shoulders and gave a light rub. "Did you ask about the sticker on the rear window of her van after I told you not to?"

Amber scowled and folded her arms. "Suzie's mom was laughing when she removed the part of the sticker just below the belt. When I asked why she didn't just remove the whole sticker and replace it with a new one she looked at me funny and then told me to mind my own business and leave."

Dale knelt down in front of Amber. "Well I'm so glad that she sent you home so that I can say goodbye to you before I go to see Amanda."

Amber smiled. "You're going to see Amanda?"

"Yes, and I am going to propose when I see her."

Amber gave a squeal of delight and hugged Dale. "Amanda will say yes when you ask. I just know it."

Dale glanced at his watch as he joined Wade in the car. It was going to be a lot tighter schedule than he had hoped it would be but barring unforeseen circumstances he should have no problem catching his flight. Dale reached into his pocket. "What do I owe you for the cab?"

Wade held up his hand and stopped Dale from removing the wallet from his pocket. "It was my treat when I sent the cab driver on his way. You didn't seem too pleased with the driver when you arrived and he looked like he wasn't too fond of you either."

Dale grinned. "Was my displeasure that obvious?"

Wade nodded. "Yes it was. So what did he do to upset you?"

Dale played with his watch as he looked out of the window at the historic buildings that lined the highway. "The man should be a tour guide. I was in a hurry and he took nothing but detours while giving commentary about the area and its attractions."

Wade checked for traffic in his rear view mirror and did a shoulder check before he changed lanes. "So what are your plans when you take Amanda out for her birthday?" Wade smiled. "I would have asked before we left the house but there wasn't enough time for you to answer all of the questions. As it is you might already be cutting it close due to the extra time you might need to clear security."

Dale looked at Wade. "What makes you say that?"

Wade stopped at an intersection and waited for the light to change. "The airports are on a heightened alert status since there was another threat made to the airlines this morning."

Dale leaned back in the seat and watched the traffic signs go by. "I should be okay but if I need to I might just have to flash my credentials." They drove in silence a few minutes before Dale spoke. "Is that job offer you keep teasing me with still open or are you just being polite by asking?"

Wade glanced at Dale. "My job offer is a standing offer, just let me know when you are ready to start." He paused, "So does this mean that you are giving the offer some thought?"

Dale played with the coin in his hand by making it move across the back of his fingers. "Yes I am giving the offer some thought, but right now my focus is on the business at hand, I have to catch this flight so that I can be where I need to be." A smile came to Dale's face as he finished his thought. "I need to be with Amanda on her birthday."

Wade merged the car onto the freeway. "Well let me know, the offer is always good and we would all like to have you closer to family." Wade found a gap in the traffic and changed lanes to avoid being stuck behind a line of slow-moving vehicles. "So what are your plans when you get home?"

Dale smiled. "I plan on seeing Amanda." He paused. "Did I happen to mention that I plan on seeing Amanda?" there was a twinkle in his eye. "I plan on seeing Amanda and hopefully I won't have to do anything that will end my current career by me landing in jail."

Wade turned his head towards Dale. "Say what?"

Dale gave Wade a reassuring wink. "I plan to propose to Amanda as soon as I see her and will do whatever it takes to make it happen; even if it means being undiplomatic towards a fellow diplomat if he gets in my way."

"Sounds like a plan to me." Wade pulled the car past the line of slower vehicles and then changed lanes to get out of the way of some cars whose drivers felt like exceeding the speed limit more than Wade was doing. "For the plan to work you need to catch this flight." Wade waited for the last speeding cars to pass and then pulled back into the lane behind them.

Dale leaned forward in his seat. "Exactly, this entire trip is going to be a precision operation with little or no room for error. I need to make all of the planned connections. That way when I land it will be early enough in the day that I will be able to pick up the engagement ring from my apartment, before I take Amanda out for her birthday."

Wade nodded his head in agreement. "It sounds like a good plan but I must warn you that if Amanda is anything like your sister, she won't go out on the town without freshening up first."

Dale looked at the exit sign and relaxed when he checked his watch. Wade had made up a lot of time. "I have considered that possibility. If all else fails, I will drop down on one knee in her living room very romantic like and propose. The important part of this plan is that I propose."

Wade smiled. "Don't you mean to say that the most important part of this plan is for Amanda to say yes?"

Dale laughed. "That would be a good thing I guess."

Soon the car came to a stop in front of the departure terminal and Wade removed Dale's bags from the trunk before closing the trunk lid "Do you want me to wait for you until I know that you made your flight?"

"That won't be necessary." Dale placed the carry bag strap over his shoulder. "If I miss this flight and lose the opportunity to be with Amanda and propose on her birthday I might be terrible company."

Wade waited until Dale was in the airport and out of sight before he pulled away from the curb and returned home.

Dale checked his suitcase and got his boarding pass before he made his way to the security checkpoint. He followed his usual pre-flight routine and drained the last of the water from his bottle before placing it into his carry bag. The phone, his wallet and his electronics were placed in a clear plastic bag for inspection. The line through the security screening during this heightened alert went slower than usual and Dale was becoming more nervous and apprehensive with each passing minute. Thanks to Wade's driving Dale still had time before his flight but he couldn't shake the concern that with this unexpected delay he might be cutting it too close for comfort. Dale was becoming a bundle of nerves at the prospects of missing the flight and another delay with the person in front of him didn't help as he could feel his anxiety growing. When it was his turn to pass through screening he placed his carryon bag in a tray on the conveyor belt feeding the scanning machine. With his passport and his boarding pass in hand Dale approached the metal detector. It was finally his turn and he walked through the metal detector as fast as he could and waited for his bag to clear the scanning machine. The operators ran the bag through the machine forward and back several times as they studied the screen. A quick hand gesture to a supervisor soon had Dale and his bag in a small room away from the inspection area for a more thorough inspection.

Dale was curious about the unexpected concern for his bag but felt no reason to worry, other than this delay might make this flight leave without him ruining the chance to propose to Amanda on her birthday. He wasn't worried about a problem with his bag because he had gone through airport security many times and his bag was packed the same way it always was. Dale sat on the chair where he had been told to sit while they examined the bag. After a few minutes a burly man in uniform looked up from Dale's bag and scowled at Dale. "Why were you so nervous going through security?"

"I wasn't nervous." Dale said firmly.

The man came near enough that when he leaned close to Dale's face it was easy to tell that the man had eaten an egg salad sandwich with onions for lunch, and possibly a clove of garlic. "No, you were acting nervous as if you were planning to do something that requires the knife concealed in your carryon bag."

The comment surprised Dale. "There is no knife in my bag."

"Our scan has revealed a knife concealed in your bag." He leaned menacingly close and stared at Dale. "Where is it?"

Dale was not going to be intimidated by the man and spoke in a voice that was emphatic and firm. "There is no knife in my bag and you are going to make me miss my flight."

The man was unwavering. "You are staying right here until we find the knife."

Dale tried to figure out what to make of this situation. "You actually think that there is a knife concealed in my bag?"

"The scanner doesn't lie."

Dale took a deep breath. "May I help you go through my bag?"

The man motioned for Dale to approach the table and Dale started to unpack his bag to show that there was no knife. The only thing he didn't open was the gift for Amanda from Jason and Vicki, but he rolled the package and flexed it like a soft cover book to show that it had no solid steel object like a knife inside. Finally, in an attempt to resolve the situation he removed the paper from the gift. As expected it was nothing more than a soft cover book with a bookmark to match the design on the cover. Dale was speechless as everyone examined the book mark. The bookmark was made of aluminum foil and cut in a shape to resemble the ornate knife on the book cover.

As Dale repacked his bag and left the book mark with the officers he couldn't help wonder if the bookmark was an innocent oversight or if Jason had deliberately placed it in the book as an ill timed practical joke. Now was not the time to find the truth but he would eventually find out.

Dale's lungs were burning as he sprinted across the airport terminal to the assigned boarding gate. The look in his eyes showed desperation as he looked at the closed door leading to the boarding tunnel and the airline staff preparing to leave the gate.

Dale set his bags on the floor and gasped for air. "Am I too late?"

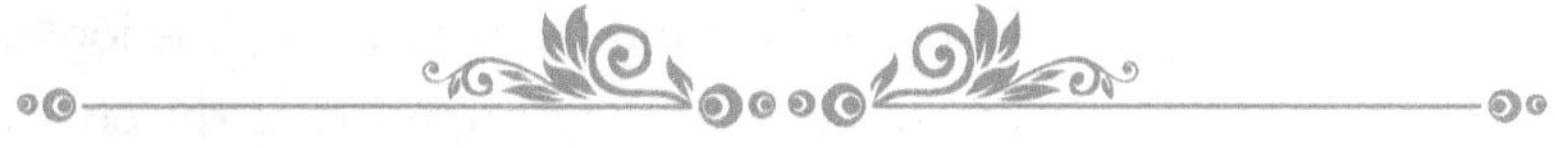

CHAPTER ELEVEN

The day had been hectic and Amanda welcomed the chance to turn off her work station and return home. She grabbed her purse and headed for the door.

Trish reached the door first and held it open for Amanda. "Are you going to be speaking with Dale tonight?"

Amanda was surprised to have Trish leave work with her since Trish normally left work with Judy. "I hope Dale calls every night but tonight I would be surprised if he calls because he might be busy with last minute preparations before leaving on his next assignment."

Trish pushed the next heavy door open as they walked towards the elevator. "Wouldn't it be wonderful if Dale calls tonight and surprises you with a marriage proposal?" Trish pushed the elevator call button and as they waited for the elevator to arrive Trish crossed the fingers of both hands. "Here's hoping he calls. My prayers are with you."

Amanda was getting tired of the recent constant reminders from her friends and coworkers that she was still a free woman. She was gracious and thanked Trish for thinking of her and Dale. Once in her apartment Amanda kicked off her shoes and sprawled across the couch. She placed her feet on the coffee table and laid her head on the afghan draped along the back of the couch. Amanda lay motionless a few moments before she reached for her journal.

A well worn envelope was now inserted with the ribbon as a bookmark to mark the page. She opened the journal and wrote the date at the top of the page as she thought about what to write. She looked at the envelope a few moments and placed the ribbon inside the envelope. Tomorrow was her birthday, the day she had been hoping to spend with Dale. She was still hopeful that he would make it, but deep inside she knew better, he was going to be on his way to an assignment that was far from here. He must have known that he couldn't make it when he had told her to have a good time for her birthday without him. She knew that she would probably spend the evening alone at home while he was being stranded in an airport who knows where. She started to write.

Today started with another bouquet of flowers – with no card again. I don't know what to think. I would like to think that all of these flowers are from Dale. But if they aren't from him, who are they from? I am beginning to think that Adam is behind the mystery of the flowers but I am afraid to ask. Am I afraid that he did send them, or more afraid that he didn't send the flowers and there is another man out there waiting to make a play for my heart? Dale is still the man who holds the key to my heart, but I can't wait for him forever. I don't want to consider this option, but at the same time I must prepare my heart for the potential disappointment of having to move on from Dale.

She looked at the framed picture of Dale and softly pleaded. "Are you ever going to propose?"

The following morning Amanda started her day in the usual fashion, a small breakfast of cold cereal and a glass of orange juice. She considered calling in sick to have a personal day for her birthday but thought better of it because work afforded her the distraction from a day alone thinking of Dale. She climbed into the shower and pampered herself by taking an extra ten minutes enjoying the warm water cascading over her body. Amanda selected Dale's favorite outfit to wear for the day. She knew that it was highly unlikely Dale was going to be there for her birthday, but she still had to look good for him, just in case he was able to make it.

Waiting for Amanda when she arrived at work was another bouquet of flowers that was more impressive than any of the others she had received up until now. She looked for a card with the flowers and wasn't surprised when there was no card; but she did find a small box of chocolates instead. She opened the chocolates and this time she found a small card with an inscription. *Here are some sweets for a special lady on her birthday.*

Amanda was appreciative for the flowers but felt disappointed to once again find no clue about who had sent the flowers.

Amanda placed the new flowers in the last open space on her desk. "This place is looking like a flower shop." Amanda declared as she sat down on her chair.

The phone rang and Amanda had to move some of the flowers so she could answer the phone. Her pulse raced in anticipation as she lifted the receiver to her ear, only to hear a dial tone. Several thoughts raced through her mind, all of them about Dale. Is he at the airport trying to call and his phone battery died? Is he at a different airport having problems making the connections? As the thoughts began to be darker in nature the phone rang again. Amanda lifted the receiver to her ear hoping that it was Dale. "Hello?" she said and then listened to the message.

"Happy birthday to you – Happy birthday to you – Happy birthday dear Amanda - Happy birthday to you."

Amanda smiled as she listened to the greeting and recognized the voices. "Thank you Wade, Gail, Amber and Jason."

"You're welcome. I hope you are having a great birthday so far." Gail said with excitement in her voice.

"So far the day is going good." Amanda leaned back in her chair wondering if she should say what she really felt.

Gail spoke again. "Did you get the flowers we sent you from Dale? He was busy and asked us to send them for him."

Amanda felt a sense of relief come over her. The flowers were from Dale. "Yes, I have received all of them."

"All of them?" Gail sounded puzzled.

"Yes, I received all of them. My desk looks like a flower shop."

"How many flowers have you received?" Gail asked cautiously.

Amanda's relief was replaced by curiosity. "How many bouquets did you send?"

"We sent one bouquet from Dale last week and one bouquet from us for your birthday. Why?"

Amanda licked her lips. "Did the flowers you sent today have a small box of chocolates?"

"I don't think so." There was a pause with muffled conversation as Gail called her children back to her side and asked them some questions. There was laughter in her voice when she started to speak. "It would seem that I need to be more careful with my account at the flower shop. Jason sent you a bunch of flowers. Amber sent you two because she really likes you so in total we have sent you five bunches of flowers that I am aware of." There was silence. "How many bunches of flowers have you received?"

"Seven."

Gail sounded upbeat. "Maybe Dale sent a couple of bouquets himself because he missed you so much?"

"Maybe he did. I will ask him when I see him."

The call ended and Amanda was relieved to know that most of the flowers, if not all of them, were from Dale and his family. Even though Dale had no idea how many flowers were sent and there were no cards with any of them. She looked at the last bouquet with the chocolates and could only wonder who they were from. She told herself they were from Dale to put her mind at ease and went back to work.

Adam called her to the office and asked her to close the door before he began speaking. "Is Dale going to be here for your birthday?"

Amanda was unsure how to answer and hesitated ever so briefly. "Probably not, but a girl can always hope for a miracle."

Adam smiled. "I'm sure that if Dale could be here with you today he would be." Adam set down his pen and closed the desk drawer while he continued speaking. "If Dale doesn't get here, it would be a shame not to celebrate another milestone of your life. I feel that a birthday needs to be celebrated and not just tolerated sitting alone at home."

Amanda was unsure where Adam was going with his comment and wanted clarity. "What are you saying?"

Adam placed his hands palm down on the desk and started to stand. "I'm saying that if Dale isn't here to celebrate your birthday with you, may I be so bold as to invite you to be my guest for the evening?"

Amanda thought about the offer a moment. "I would be happy to be your guest." she surprised herself at how quickly she responded and then added. "But only if Dale doesn't make it back in time."

Adam's smile grew. "Great, I look forward to maybe spending some time with you this evening."

Amanda chuckled. "Thank you for caring enough to maybe spend time with me." She looked at the clock. "Is it okay if I leave early? I would like to take some of these flowers home and will need to make more than one trip."

"Of course you may." Adam came out from behind the desk. "In fact let me help you take those flowers to your home."

Before Amanda could move to leave the office, Adam grabbed his jacket and escorted her to her desk and took two of the larger bouquets in his arms. "Janet, Amanda is taking the rest of the day off and I will be out for awhile helping her take these flowers to her home. If Dale phones, tell him where Amanda is."

Dale looked at the display on his phone. He was not a happy man after the fiasco with the book mark at security had almost made him miss the flight. Dale breathed a sigh of relief when he was on the airplane but his smile had vanished when saw that he was going to spend the flight wedged like a sardine between two very large people.

Dale stood in front of the girl at the ticket counter in the next airport trying to find a suitable flight to start his detour to see Amanda. He had already purchased a ticket on a different flight but had been bumped from the flight because some wealthy sheik had decided to bring his wife, and his other wife, and another wife along with all their children on that particular flight. Money talks and his had screamed loud enough that Dale and a few other passengers had to find another flight. He checked the departure times and made the mental calculations as to when he would arrive. He purchased his ticket. If all worked well without any more delays there was still a chance for him to propose to Amanda on her birthday. It may not be at her favorite restaurant, or in any perfect setting he had imagined, but if it had to be – her living room would have to do. Even if he had to wake her, it was time to put a ring on Amanda's finger... today!

Dale purchased a candy bar and a bottle of water before he took a seat to wait for the flight. He remembered arriving for Ramón and Consuela's wedding and finding his phone battery was dead so he resisted the urge to pass the time playing games on his phone. He wanted to surprise Amanda with his arrival for her birthday but couldn't wait to hear her voice. He moved around the airport until he found a strong signal and decided to call Amanda to wish her a happy birthday. He dialed her work number. With each ring the anticipation of hearing her voice brought him joy.

"Hello?"

"Amanda?" Dale wasn't sure if it was Amanda because of the noise in the background.

"No, this is Janet."

"Hi Janet, this is Dale. May I please speak with Amanda?"

"I'm sorry but she isn't here, she took the afternoon off but you can reach her at home."

Dale was disappointed that Amanda hadn't answered his call but liked the prospects of a longer conversation. "Thank you Janet. I will call her at home."

Dale was about to make the call when a large group of young people entered the airport with their phones and devices and the signal strength dropped to where he was unable to make the call. When there was finally a strong enough signal Dale dialed Amanda's home phone.

"Hello?"

Dale's heart sank. The voice on the phone was that of the annoying Adam, the mystery man who claimed to be his competition for Amanda's heart, and now he was at Amanda's in the middle of the day – on her birthday. "Who is this?"

"Who are you?" Adam replied.

"This is Dale Evers and I would like to speak with Amanda." Dale struggled to control his desire to yell at this interloper who it seemed was trying to come between him and Amanda. "Why are you at her apartment in the middle of the day?"

"I'm at her apartment because I helped her bring a few things home from the office."

Dale took a deep breath. "And why are you answering her phone?"

"Amanda is in the bathroom and would be devastated if she knew that she missed your call so I answered it for her."

"Tell Amanda that I am on the phone. I don't have a lot of time before I have to board the plane."

Adam seemed in no hurry to grant Dale's request to speak with Amanda and kept asking questions that annoyed Dale. "So is it good weather for the flight to your next assignment?"

Dale could scarcely contain his outrage as he used all of his restraint to remain civil and answer the questions. "The weather is great with clear blue skies; a perfect day to fly if I don't get bumped. Where is Amanda?"

Adam seemed to delight in the situation as he fueled the fire within Dale. "Now it would seem that Amanda is busy in the other room watering the many bouquets of flowers from her secret admirers."

Dale was surprised to hear about secret admirers and it showed in his voice. "Flowers from her what?"

Adam must have picked up on the frustration and kept teasing Dale. "Her secret admirers, it would seem that you are taking too long to propose and others are ready to move in to sweep her off of her feet." He paused. "Did you know that your coworkers have even started an office pool for when you will propose to Amanda?"

"They did what?"

"They started an office pool." There was a mocking tone in Adam's voice.

The thought that his delay in proposing to Amanda had made them the target of an office pool hurt Dale. It wouldn't be the perfect setting he had planned but he was ready to propose to Amanda over the phone that very instant. His voice was firm as he spoke. "Let me speak with Amanda."

Adam was enjoying making Dale frustrated. "I told you that Amanda was busy with the flowers and can't come to the phone right now. Shall I have her return your call when she has finished?"

Dale snapped. "And when would that be, next year?"

There was a sneer in Adam's voice. "I wouldn't make you wait that long. I'll tell her that you called later tonight after I have taken her to the movies and then to her favorite restaurant to celebrate her birthday. Would that be soon enough?"

Dale gagged with rage and was unable to speak.

Adam continued. "Dale this evening feels like it would be the perfect time to propose to Amanda. I can't think of a more perfect setting than to make her happy in her favorite restaurant." There was a pause. "In fact I think I might...." There was a click and the line went dead.

Dale was unsure if his phone had died or if he had hung up on again. Dale was upset and could scarcely contain the rage building up inside as he yelled at the phone. "Over my dead body will you propose to Amanda tonight, you jerk!" Dale tried to call back but there was no signal. Dale stuffed the phone into his pocket. He was a man possessed as he began a more desperate search checking for earlier flights of any kind that would get him to Amanda before he lost her forever.

Imagination can be a terrible thing when you are thinking that the worst is about to happen and right now Dale's imagination was not making him very happy. He had tried every conceivable alternative to find a faster way to get to Amanda so he could stop a terrible personal disaster from happening. It had been a valiant effort but any viable option was already sold out so Dale resigned himself to the reality of having to take the flight he was already booked on. It felt like an eternity before the boarding call for the flight was announced, but when it was,

Dale was at the front of the line. The flight left on time and Dale tried to relax until a sudden storm had the plane stuck in a holding pattern over the destination airport for a substantial length of time before it was diverted to an airport that was over an hour drive away on a good day.

Amanda put the finishing touches to her make up as she waited for Adam to arrive. She glanced at the phone and then at the clock. It wasn't like Dale to not at least call to wish her a happy birthday. She wished that Dale was there to take her out for the evening but knew that if he could have been there he would be. She reached for her journal but before she could open the book the door bell rang. Amanda opened the door to find a dozen roses being presented to her by Adam.

"An event such as this would not be complete without roses." Adam entered the room. "Do you have a vase to put them in?"

Amanda went to the kitchen and returned with a vase filled with water. The roses were arranged in the vase and set on the coffee table –the only open space left for flowers. "They are lovely but you didn't have to buy me roses."

Adam looked into Amanda's eyes. "I know that I didn't have to buy you roses. I bought them for you because I wanted to." He extended his arm to Amanda. "Shall we go celebrate your birthday?"

Amanda placed her arm in Adam's and had a twinge of guilt because it felt as if she was cheating on Dale. The feeling passed and the couple took the short stroll to the theater. The evening was enjoyable but Amanda kept looking around as if she had hoped to see Dale. After the show they walked at a leisurely pace as they made their way to the restaurant where they were seated in the table that Dale always requested.

It was getting late when Adam escorted Amanda back to her place and he waited for her to unlock the door.

Once the door was unlocked Amanda turned to Adam. "I had a lovely time tonight. Thank you."

Adam took Amanda by the hand and kissed the back of it. "I had a lovely time tonight as well. Thank you for allowing me to help you celebrate your birthday." Adam let go of Amanda's hand and stepped away from the door. "It is getting late and we both have work in the morning." Adam waited for the door to close then went on his way.

Amanda hung up her coat and sat on the couch. She kicked off her shoes and began to rub her feet. She had walked a lot further than she had planned to walk otherwise she would have worn different shoes. She moved the vase full of roses to the end of the table so that they wouldn't get knocked over when she put her feet up while she wrote in her journal.

Amanda opened her journal and placed the well worn envelope on the couch beside her. She took the pen and sat in silence as she decided what to write. She yawned and stretched her hands above her head before putting pen to paper to write the date. She then started to make the journal entry.

Today is my birthday; another mile marker along the pathway of life. This the first time in a long time that Dale has not been here to celebrate my birthday with me, in fact he never even called to wish me a happy birthday.

I would be lying if I said that I didn't enjoy this evening with Adam. He is a real gentleman who knows how to show a girl a good time. If he should ask me out again I doubt that I will hesitate to say yes since after today I promised myself that I would start looking if Dale hadn't proposed to me by my birthday.

Amanda grabbed a tissue and wiped her eyes. She looked at Dale's picture and then at the clock. "You still have time to call me on my birthday if you hurry."

Dale hung his head as he stood in the airport a dejected man. The storm was fierce between where he was and where he wanted to go. He had tried everything he could think of to get to Amanda but the winds were so strong that ground travel was not recommended and the roads were closed until further notice. If it was possible he would have walked the entire distance to Amanda's door just to put a ring on Amanda's finger. Dale was haunted by the last words he had heard from Adam where he had hinted that he might propose to Amanda today. Dale had done his best but today his best wasn't good enough. He was not a happy man. He trusted that Amada would remain true and he planned to proceed as if she did; but there was the nagging uncertainty that kept him feeling uneasy as he purchased a ticket for the only option he had left. He needed to reconnect with the flight to his new assignment.

CHAPTER TWELVE

*G*ail couldn't help but wonder if Dale had made it to Amanda in time to propose to her so that she could start planning their wedding. This wedding was going to be a highlight for the family but that wasn't the only thing on her mind. Gail was excited for Alex and Chad and looked forward to helping them with their wedding plans. She was going to be a Matron of Honor without peers. The biggest challenge she could see with planning the wedding was to stay within the strict budget Alex had set since she was intent on paying for her wedding herself. Gail wasn't too concerned about the budget and felt that with a little financial help from her and Wade they could have the glamorous wedding she envisioned for them.

Gail had just sat down with her book and put her feet up when the phone rang. Jason and Amber were home so Gail wasn't in any rush to answer the phone until she realised that her children ignored the phone and continued doing what they were doing. Gail rushed to the phone. "Hello?"

There was a familiar voice was on the other end. "Hello Mrs. Rollins, this is Mrs. Tennant."

It had been quite awhile since the two ladies had spoken. Gail had been curious about what service projects *The Angels of Mercy* had been up to, but just not curious enough to call. "Mrs. Tennant. What a pleasant surprise to hear from you." Gail could think of no service projects that needed her attention and wondered why Mrs. Tennant would be calling. They must need her help with something. "How are you and *The Angels of Mercy* doing?"

"We are doing fine. Thank you." Mrs. Tennant was polite yet short and official in her response.

"Glad to hear it."

There was little to no emotion in Mrs. Tennant's voice when she spoke. "The girls and I have a request to make of you."

"Okay, what is your request?" Gail listened to what Mrs. Tennant had to say and was shocked to learn the purpose for the call. After listening to Mrs. Tennant talk for fifteen minutes without being able to get a word in, Gail was exasperated. "So what you are telling me is that Alex and Chad have asked *The Angel's of Mercy* to plan the entire wedding for them."

"That is Correct." Mrs. Tennant sounded very matter of fact.

Gail couldn't believe what she was hearing as she questioned what she had just heard. "And my involvement in the planning will only happen if you feel that my help is needed?"

Mrs. Tennant's tone was firm. "That is correct. We, *The Angels of Mercy*, have grown close to Alex and her family and wish to do all of the planning as our gift to her. We plan to do the wedding up right and stay in budget." There was a pause. "Trust me; it is going to be a memorable event."

Gail had no doubt that the wedding would be memorable. The big question in Gail's mind was how it would be memorable. Gail's frustration started to grow with the prospects of being unable to help. How could Mrs. Tennant and *The Angels of Mercy* exclude her from the wedding planning? Gail took a deep breath. "I can help Alex with the wedding and still stay in budget."

There was a substantial pause before Mrs. Tennant spoke again. "Mrs. Rollins. Your tastes are much more extravagant than what Alex can afford. Besides, Alex is like a daughter to us and we wish to do this for her."

"Oh!" Gail felt hurt and didn't know what else to say. Alex was like a daughter to her as well and she wanted to help plan her wedding.

Mrs. Tennant started to speak again. "What day can you come past Gloria's home so she can size Amber for her bridesmaid dress?"

Gail was shocked to hear that Gloria was making the dresses. She had seen some of Gloria's handiwork and wondered if the bridesmaid dresses would stay together any better than the costumes she had made for the school drama production. Gail was already envisioning a disaster in the making and then had a horrifying thought. "Is Gloria sewing the wedding gown?"

Mrs. Tennant sounded disappointed. "Gloria offered to make the wedding gown to help save money but Alex wants to go dress shopping with her mother. If she can't find a nice dress in her price range, I am sure that she will ask Gloria to sew the wedding gown as well."

Gail was silent. It was scary enough to think how the bridal party was going to look in their dresses. A sinking feeling crept into the pit of her stomach at the thought of a sleeve falling off of one of the dresses in front of family and friends. Gail had been silent for longer than she had planned and knew that she had to say something. "Let me know when it will be a good time to see Gloria for the fitting."

"I'll check with Gloria and get back to you about the fitting." Mrs. Tennant was about to hang up when she thought of something else she wanted to say. "And another thing..."

"Yes." Gail wished the conversation was already over but remained polite as she listened to Mrs. Tennant.

"Don't think that you have to worry about a thing, everything is under control and Martha is taking care of the meal. Goodbye."

Gail hung up the phone and sat in silence as she contemplated the impending disaster that would forever be part of the memories known as Alex and Chad's wedding. She never had much time to dwell on her concerns for the wedding before the phone rang again.

Gail debated whether to answer the phone. She wondered if it was Mrs. Tennant with something else she had forgotten to say to further ruin her day. On the fifth ring Gail reached for the phone. There was no emotion in her voice when she answered. "Hello?"

In contrast the voice on the other end was upbeat and happy. "Gail this is Alex."

Gail felt an instant improvement in her mood and it reflected in her voice. "Hi Alex, what's up?"

"I was wondering if you and Amber would be able to come shopping with me and my mother today."

Gail loved spending time with Alex and welcomed the opportunity to be involved with her family. "Certainly, what are we shopping for?"

"My mother and I are looking for wedding gowns and we would really like you and Amber to join us."

Gail was excited at being invited to shop for the wedding gown. After speaking with Mrs. Tennant, Gail had all but resigned herself to her role as a Matron of Honor whose only responsibility would be to stand in the reception line. "We would love to go shopping with you. Can we come past your house and pick you up?"

"You don't have to, but if you would like to come get us in one hour that would be fine."

"We'll be there." Gail hung up the phone and called Amber. "Sweetheart we need to get ready to leave."

Amber took a while to answer. "Why do we have to leave?"

Gail was already in her coat and reaching for her car keys. "We are going wedding dress shopping with Alex and her mother."

Without another word Amber had her coat on and was at Gail's side.

During the drive to the wedding store Gail wanted to confirm what Mrs. Tennant had told her earlier. "Alex, I was wondering if you are okay with the way that *The Angels of Mercy* is taking over the planning of your wedding."

Alex hesitated a few moments and glanced at her mother. "At first it bothered me a lot that they were taking over like they did."

"Then why are you letting them?"

Alex licked her lips. "I didn't want to hurt their feelings when I saw how happy it made them to help. Besides they have done so much for our family."

Gail remembered conversations she had with Vicki about the reception food. "I thought that Vicki was doing the food for you."

"She is doing the food for me."

Gail was confused. "But Mrs. Tennant said that Martha is doing the food."

"And she is doing the food as well."

Gail looked at Alex in the rear-view mirror. "I don't understand how that is going to work."

Alex smiled. "Martha is going to make a dessert that I decided to have her make."

Gail was curious. "How did you decide what dessert she should make? I've tasted some of her cooking."

Amber joined the conversation. "Is Martha the lady who baked the cookies that chipped daddy's tooth?"

Gail could feel an uncomfortable blush coming. "Yes sweetheart, but hush."

Alex's mother spoke. "Of all the things that Martha cooked for the family when I was sick, she made this dish four times and it was always good. Plus it is inexpensive to make so it will fit into the budget."

Amber had been told to keep her questions to herself but she couldn't stay quiet any longer. "So how is Vicki going to do the food for the reception when Martha is doing it?"

Alex gave a wry smile. "Angelo's is catering other events that day and will bring the *leftovers* from a cancelled party that will only end up in the garbage if they can't be used."

Gail thought about the plan then nodded her approval. "Smart, Martha can't stand seeing good food go to waste so she should be more than willing to add Angelo's treats to the table."

Amber was just getting started with her questions. "Is Martha going to make the wedding cake?"

Alex answered. "The wedding cake is going to be made by my future sister in law."

"Who is decorating the church hall for the wedding?" Amber's next question came without hesitation.

"Mrs. Tennant has some friends who have enough decorations to do the church hall."

Amber filled the rest of the drive time with a barrage of questions. As the car was pulling into the parking lot of the dress store Amber asked one final question. "Where are you and Chad going on your honeymoon?"

Alex looked into Amber's eyes. "We are not going on a honeymoon."

The look on Amber's face was one of disbelief. "Everyone needs to go on a honeymoon, right mommy."

Gail put the car in park. "I'm sure that Alex and Chad are going on a honeymoon. Sometimes people like to keep where they are going a secret." Gail glanced towards Alex. "Isn't that right Alex?"

Alex nodded. "Yes it is."

Inside the store the small group of shoppers began looking at the numerous racks of dresses and admiring the ones being displayed on the mannequins. The salesgirl was attentive to what styles had caught their attention and selected several wedding gowns for Alex to try on. She helped Alex try on the first dress selected and brought her out for all to see. Alex looked stunning. The dress was perfect and not a single alteration would be required.

"What do you think of the dress?" Alex asked while looking in the full length mirrors.

Her mother was the first to comment as she motioned for Alex to turn again. "The dress is lovely. It is all that I could have imagined your wedding dress would be."

Alex looked to Gail. "What do you think?"

Gail gave Alex thumbs up. "There appears to be no reason to try on any other dress. I think the shopping part of this trip is over."

Amber clasped her hands together. "You should buy the dress."

Alex turned to the salesgirl. "How much is the dress?"

The salesgirl revealed the price and Alex gulped. "That is more than I had budgeted for." She turned and looked at her reflection one more time then sighed. "We need to look at more dresses."

Several more beautiful dresses were tried on but none with the stunning effect of the first one. It was easy to see that Alex was not as excited with any of the other dresses she tried on. It saddened Gail to see the look of disappointment grow on Alex's face after every dress she tried on.

Gail knew that the first dress was the one for Alex but she hesitated to speak up because she knew that Alex was determined to stay in budget. She could remain silent no longer. "Alex. Would you allow me to pay the difference above your budget, as our wedding gift to you, so that you can have that dress for your wedding?"

Alex was slow to respond as she contemplated the offer but when she did respond there was a resolve in her voice. "Thank you so much for the offer but I couldn't."

Gail looked at Alex and her mother. "It would be our pleasure to help out in this small way."

Tears started forming in Alex's eyes. "You and Wade have already done so much for us that I would feel bad if I took advantage of your kindness and generosity."

Gail sat back to watch Alex narrow her choices until she had settled for a nice looking dress that fit her budget. After finalizing all the details for the payment plan the dress was put on layaway. It saddened Gail that Alex had turned down the offer to help pay for the dress that looked so perfect but it was her choice and now the dress shopping was completed.

Alex and her mother were delivered home, and then after a few more errands Gail and Amber returned home. Gail was making her favorite pasta sauce for the evening meal when Amber came into the kitchen with her piggy bank. The appearance of the piggy bank surprised Gail since the piggy bank always came out on allowance day, but today wasn't that day.

"What's up sweetheart?" Gail was curious as she watched Amber set the piggy bank onto the table and then climb onto a chair. Trying to guess what was going on in that pretty little head was usually a bad idea so Gail waited for Amber to tell her what she was thinking.

Amber was silent as she played with the piggy bank by sliding it from side to side while she rotated it. After a few moments of silence Amber was ready to share her thoughts. "Mommy?"

"Yes dear?" Gail felt certain that Amber was going to ask for some of the pretty new fish they had seen in the pet store. She had been wrong to make that assumption and her heart melted when Amber revealed what was on her mind.

Amber slid the piggy bank across the table towards Gail. "I want to help buy the dress that we both know Alex should have for her wedding."

Gail saw the intent in Amber's eyes and felt helpless. "I want to help pay for the dress too but Alex said that she didn't want any of my money to pay for that dress."

Amber looked serious with her pursed lips and a cute scowl on her face as she placed her hands palms down on the table. "She said that she didn't want any of your money, but Alex never said that I couldn't help."

Gail was impressed by Amber's willingness to help and her creativity to find a solution. "I'm glad that you want to help pay for the dress but it will cost more than the money you have saved from your allowance."

Amber folded her arms and stared at Gail. "I know it will, but if you help me pay for the dress I won't ask for any of my allowance until the dress is paid for."

Feelings of pride for this selfless gesture began to swell up inside Gail. "Why do you want to do this for Alex?"

The arms were unfolded and the hands were once again placed palms down on the table as Amber leaned forward. "Alex needs to have that dress and I really like her."

Gail blinked away a tear as she looked at Amber. "Alex having that dress for her wedding means that much to you?" Gail watched the curly blonde hair bounce as Amber nodded her head to the affirmative. "Well then, I will see what I can do."

Amber slid from the chair and gave Gail a hug. "I love you mommy. You're the best." She then took her piggy bank from the table and left the kitchen.

CHAPTER THIRTEEN

Gail had not heard a word from Dale since he left to see Amanda on her birthday and the suspense was killing her. She wanted to know what had happened and if there was going to be a wedding in the near future, but if Dale hadn't proposed she didn't want to be the one to spoil the moment. Gail figured that she could use Alex's wedding as an indirect way to talk wedding without coming right out and asking if Dale had proposed. She picked up the phone and was ready to call when the reminder chimed on her phone. *Gloria's for dress measuring.* Gail set her phone down and reached for the phone on the desk. It may not be the normal length of call but she had to know if Dale had proposed, and more importantly if Amanda had said yes. She dialed the number.

Amanda answered on the second ring. "Hello?"

"Hi Amanda its Gail, I had a few minutes before I have to take Amber to get fitted for her bridesmaid dress so I thought I would give you a call to see how you are doing." She paused. "So how are you doing?

Amanda sighed. "Okay I guess. I haven't seen Dale since before he left for Consuela's wedding."

"He has called you though, right?"

"Yes he has, but whoever said that long distance phone calls and sending flowers was the next best thing to being there was a fool. You can't hug a rose because of the thorns and the phone keeps disconnecting when you hold it close."

Gail laughed. "I remember saying the part about the flowers when he found out that he might not see you on your birthday."

"So he said." Amanda shared a laugh with Gail before she asked. "Whose wedding is Amber going to be a bridesmaid at?"

"Alex and Chad's wedding."

There was silence before Amanda spoke again. "Alex is a girl right?"

Gail laughed. "Yes Alex is a girl. Her full name is Alexandria. She goes by Alex because it is short."

Amanda chuckled. "If Alex wasn't a girl you would have a lot of explaining to do to Amber."

"No kidding." Gail wanted to talk longer but she had to take Amber to Gloria's for measurements. "Well I'm glad that things are going well for you and I hope that Dale can get back to you soon. I'll call you back another time."

They ended the call and Gail could only wonder what had happened to keep Dale from Amanda on her birthday because he had planned it out to the last detail. Now was not the time to dwell on it because she had a bridesmaid that needed to be measured for a dress.

True to her word Gail arrived at Gloria's home with Amber. Gloria led them to the sewing room at the back of the house and was excited to start making the dresses for the wedding.

Gloria motioned for Amber to step up onto a stool and took out her measuring tape. "I am so glad that you could make it today on such short notice."

Gail took a seat and watched Gloria take the first measurement. "Our schedules matched perfectly. Almost like us getting together today was meant to be."

Amber squirmed when Gloria took the next measurement. "That tickles."

In no time at all Gloria had all the measurements she needed to make Amber's dress and told Amber to take the seat beside her mother while motioning for Gail to come forward. "Now I need to take your measurements so that I can make your Matron of Honor dress."

Gail hesitated as the memories of the failed drama costumes flashed in her head. She did not want a wardrobe malfunction to upstage the bride and groom. "Are you sure that you will have enough time to make the extra dress? I already have a very nice dress at home in my closet that will serve my needs nicely."

Gloria once again motioned for Gail to come forward. "Let me take your measurements right now so that I have them on file. If making your dress proves to be too much for me I will let you know. Otherwise it will be my pleasure to make a dress for you." Gloria stepped aside. "So please let me take your measurements."

Gail took her place to allow Gloria to take her measurements and only questioned the accuracy of the measurements a couple of times when the numbers sounded too big. When all the measuring was complete it was time to leave but Gail had seen some dresses on a rack that caught her eye. Maybe she was being too hasty to question how the dresses would turn out. She pointed to the rack of dresses. "Did you make all of those dresses?"

"Yes I did. Would you like to see them?"

"If I may, they look like designer dresses."

Gloria beamed. "They are copies that I made for myself."

Gail examined the dresses and soon felt excited to see what the dresses for the wedding were going to turn out like. "These are gorgeous and I can hardly wait to see what magic you do for the wedding."

"Thank you."

Amber led the way back to the front door and was surprised to find Vicky on the front step ready to ring the doorbell when she opened it. "Hi Vicky." Amber reached out to hug Vicky.

Vicky leaned down to give Amber a hug. "Hi Amber, did you just get measured for your bridesmaid dress?"

Amber stepped back. "Yes I did and so did mommy."

Vicky stepped aside and allowed Amber and Gail to exit before she entered the house to join Gloria.

Wade greeted his favorite girls with a hug. Amber returned the hug and left for her room. Gail's hug ended with a kiss and a question. "What were you planning to have for the evening meal?"

Gail pulled away and smiled. "I thought that you would have asked how things went at Gloria's."

Wade took Gail's coat. "I'm curious to find out how that went as well, but what were you planning for tonight's meal?"

"I was planning to have the lasagna that is in the oven cooking." Gail looked towards the kitchen and sniffed the air. "Did something happen to the lasagna?" She started walking towards the kitchen. "It doesn't smell burnt."

Wade joined Gail in the kitchen where she was greeted by the sight of several dishes on the table. She surveyed the kitchen and shook her head as she picked up the empty pan that used to hold the lasagna. She placed the dish in the sink and reached for the bowl with a sliver of crouton in the bottom and smelled like Caesar salad. "What happened?"

Wade tossed the empty salad dressing bottle into the garbage container and started to put the dirty dishes into the dishwasher. "Jason and a few of his friends stopped in for a snack after basketball."

"That was more than a snack. The lasagna was large enough to feed us for a couple of meals." Gail placed the last glass into the dishwasher and closed the door. She opened the refrigerator. "They used five heads of lettuce for the salad." She looked at Wade. "They ate all of the garlic bread as well."

"So it would seem." Wade put his arm around Gail's shoulder. "I think that it would be fitting to go out tonight and eat at Jason's favorite restaurant without him." Wade smiled. "Then we should bring home a small doggy bag and put it in the refrigerator."

"Why would we bring him anything?"

Wade rubbed Gail's shoulders. "It would be like eating potato chips. One is never enough because you always want more. So if the doggy bag is too small to satisfy it will drive him crazy."

Gail kissed Wade. "You're mean and I like it." Gail closed the refrigerator door and called for Amber.

CHAPTER FOURTEEN

It was time for Gail and the bridesmaids to meet with Gloria to try on the dresses. The first person to try on her dress was Amber. Gail was impressed by how well the dress fit her little angel. For lack of a better word she thought that the dress looked perfect.

Now it was time for Gail to try on her dress. Before she put it on Gail inspected the seams for stability and breathed a sigh of relief. She just might have to return the backup dress she had purchased, or maybe not because it was a nice dress. Pulling the dress over her head Gail winced in pain. There was a pin hidden in the seam under her arm. Gail removed the pin and once again pulled the dress over her head. She looked at her reflection in the mirror. The dress looked nice but Gail felt that it hung too loose in the areas that she had questioned Gloria about the measurements.

Gail joined the others to model her dress.

Gloria checked the fit and made a few notes for the alterations she needed to make. "It would seem that you have lost some weight since the initial measuring. This part of the dress seems a bit loose and needs to be adjusted." Gloria placed a few pins and told Gail to change out of the dress.

The next dress to be fitted was Vicky's. She modeled for Gloria who once again made notes for some alterations needed to lower the unnatural height that the dress held her womanly attributes. Other than that the dress hung proper and looked lovely.

Next it was Sandy's turn to try on her dress. She modeled the dress and Gloria took notes. "Well my dear it would seem that you have lost some weight. I will need to adjust the shoulder straps and raise the bodice." Gloria grabbed the side seams. "I will take in the sides to make it more form fitting and you will be all set."

The girls went outside and Gail stayed back to speak with Gloria. "Thank you for all that you have done to help with Alex's wedding."

Gloria placed the alteration notes onto the hangers with the dresses. "It is my pleasure to do it for her. She is a lovely young lady."

"Yes she is a lovely young lady." Gail paused. "If there s anything that I can do to help with the dresses just let me know. I am always willing to help."

"Thank you for the offer but everything is under control." Gloria motioned towards the door and they joined the girls outside.

Gail drove away from Gloria's with a sense of relief that the bridesmaid dresses were looking so good.

Gail and Amber accepted Alex's invitation to join her family at the dress shop for the final fitting of the wedding gown. As they waited for Alex to make her appearance in the gown Amber visited with Alex's sisters while Gail talked with Alex's mother. "Well Carol, are you getting excited about the big day?"

Carol gave a small sigh. "Yes and no."

Gail wondered what reservations Carol could have. "Yes and no?"

Carol wrung her hands. "I'm excited for Alex and Chad and I hope the day will be all they want it to be."

"So what part of the wedding are you not excited about?"

Carol leaned close to Gail and spoke softly. "I fear that Alex has put too much trust in Mrs. Tennant and *The Angels of Mercy* for planning the wedding and that she might be disappointed."

Gail felt that she knew how Carol was feeling about the Angels of Mercy and wanted to put her mind at ease. "Gloria is doing a wonderful job on the bridesmaid dresses and once the final alterations are done I'm sure that they will be spectacular." Gail wondered if her review about the dresses may have been too glowing but it was too late. The words were out.

"Do you really think so?"

Gail saw the relief in Carol's eyes. "Amber's dress is perfect and needed no alterations."

Carol sighed. "That is a relief."

Just then Alex entered the room wearing the wedding dress and she looked beautiful.

Carol held her hand to her mouth and gasped. "Alexandria Timpson you look gorgeous."

The dress was perfect in every way as Alex turned to model the dress and to look at her reflection in the large mirrors surrounding the room. Alex stopped turning when she faced Gail and stood motionless except for the slight quiver of her chin. "The dress is gorgeous but you shouldn't have spent your money on my dress."

Before the conversation went any further Amber spoke up. "Mommy never spent any of her money on the dress."

Alex looked at Amber. "She didn't?"

Amber was beaming. "No, I spent my allowance money so that you could have this dress."

Alex reached for a tissue to wipe her eyes. "Why would you want to spend your allowance on me?"

Amber moved closer to Alex. "I did it because I love you."

Alex spoke softly with a quiver in her voice. "I love you too." Alex looked at Gail. "That girl must get a generous allowance."

Gail shrugged her shoulders. "Let's just say that she won't be getting any new fish for quite awhile."

Gloria had planned to have the final fitting for the dresses just two days before the wedding until Gail had convinced her that it should be done sooner, just in case more alterations needed to be done. Gloria had scoffed at the idea but soon relented when Gail became more insistent.

The day for the final fittings was now set to be done four days before the wedding. Amber tried on her dress and it still looked perfect so it was set aside for Gail to take home with her.

Gail tried on her dress. The dress fit better in some places but still felt too loose in others. It was a marked improvement from what it had been so Gail decided that she could live with it and not make Gloria any more work. Gail's dress was set aside to take home.

Sandy tried on her dress. Gloria was shocked to see how it looked and checked to make sure that she was trying the right dress. The top was considerably looser than the first time she had tried it on and it drooped in places that were less than flattering. The waist was resting on her hips leaving unwanted gathers around the stomach. Gloria started to make more notes and started to pin the dress to make it fit. "I have no idea how this happened unless I put the wrong alteration notes on the dresses." Gloria handed Vicky her dress and told her to try it on.

Vicky tried on her dress and came out into the room. Gail was able to keep a straight face and her urge to laugh in check to avoid hurting the feelings of Gloria and Vicky. There was Vicky with her womanly assets being held high enough to hide her necklace and close enough to touch her chin when she looked down. Instead of being expanded the side seams were tight enough to make it hard for Vicki to take a deep breath. Gloria had indeed done the wrong alterations to each dress. "Oops, I will make the alterations and have you return in two days for the final fitting." Gloria took some more notes and then checked to see what fabric she had left.

Gail could see a look of concern on Gloria's face when she had very little fabric left to work with. "Gloria I am going to leave my dress here in case you run out of fabric to fix the dresses for the girls. They need to match as bridesmaids. I have a lovely dress to wear if I need to."

"Mrs. Rollins your dress is complete and I would feel bad if I cut it up."

Gail handed the dress to Gloria. "I would feel bad if you were unable to finish the bridesmaid dresses in time. Please use this dress if you need to, this color is not a common one that can be matched on short notice."

Gloria looked as if she was ready to cry as she took the dress from Gail. "I should be fine but thank you."

Gail was concerned about the predicament but was at a loss as to what she could do to help out.

Gail drove away from Gloria's with an uneasy feeling about the bridesmaid dresses and felt that something had to be done. Gail stopped at the store where she had purchased her back up dress and made several purchases before going home.

CHAPTER FIFTEEN

Wade returned home from work and entered the kitchen for a snack to tide him over until it was time to eat. After he had returned the milk to the refrigerator Wade removed the invitation to Chad and Alex's wedding from the refrigerator door. With the invitation in hand he went to join Gail in the living room. He sat in the comfy recliner chair next to her and watched Gail read her book. He played with the invitation until he got her attention and she stopped to look at him. "Gail I do hope that you will be on your best behavior during this wedding."

Gail looked at the invitation and then gave Wade a questioning look. "And why do you think that I wouldn't be on my best behavior?"

Wade leaned forward and placed the invitation on the coffee table. "No reason."

Comments like that from Wade had purpose and Gail pushed for an answer. "There has to be a reason or you wouldn't have brought up the subject."

Wade gave a sheepish grin. "Actually there is a very good reason for me to bring it up."

"And what is this good reason?" Gail closed her book and set it on the arm of the chair.

Wade continued to grin. "I learned about part of the groom's guest list today."

Gail gave Wade her get to the point expression and followed it with a question. "What are you trying to say?"

Wade tried to be more serious but was unable to lose the grin. "Do you know much about Chad's family?"

"You know that I don't know much about his family." Gail placed her feet onto the floor and glared at Wade. "Is there something that I should know about Chad's family before the wedding?"

Wade's expression became more somber. "Nothing much except that you might not like all of his family."

Gail was losing her patience with this vague conversation. "So what members of Chad's family do I know well enough not to like?"

Wade held his hand to his ear like a phone. "Thank you for calling the offices of Shyster, Shyster and Dufus."

Gail's jaw dropped and her expression changed to one of disbelief. "Chad is too nice to belong to that family."

Wade pretended to hang up his phone. "It's true."

"Excuse me?"Gail's eyes narrowed. "That's not funny. Chad seems so normal."

Wade laughed out loud. "They are all normal. You just have an issue with Jack's father."

Gail's hands closed into fists and she shook them menacingly. "Yes I do have an issue with that man." She took a long slow breath. "Every time I see Mr. B. S. Crappo I want to sock him in the eye."

Wade leaned towards Gail and took her fists in his hands. "I still wouldn't recommend doing that. He is a lawyer after all."

Gail gave a big sigh and relaxed her hands until Wade could slip his fingers between hers. "You know what I mean."

Wade winked at Gail. "I know exactly what you mean, but the question still remains. When B.S. Crappo comes through the receiving line can you be gracious enough to not cause a scene?"

Gail took a moment to fantasize what she could do to B.S. Crappo in a few moments at close range. She then cleared the thoughts from her mind. "I guess I will have to." She paused. "I will do it for Alex's sake."

The wedding day arrived and Gail hoped that enough had been done by *The Angels of Mercy* to have everything in order. The reception hall was tastefully decorated and the centerpieces on the tables were delightful. Gail could think of no other touches she would make. *The Angels of Mercy* had done well.

Gloria had called the day before and told Gail that she would have to wear the other dress for the wedding because some extra material had been required for the bridesmaid dresses. Gail kept telling herself that everything was going to be fine even though she had this nagging feeling of impending doom. The bridesmaid dresses looked wonderful even though there still appeared to be a slight issue with the resting height of the girl's womanly attributes. Gail was pleased to see how excited Gloria was to tell all that would listen that she had made the bridesmaid dresses. Gloria had done well and had earned the bragging rights.

Gail had purchased several different accessories for the girl's to wear depending on how things worked out with the alterations. She had even placed several dresses on hold at the store just in case. As it turned out the only thing needed was a distraction to help draw attention from the height issues with the dresses. It was a warm day but neither Vicki nor Sandy had an issue with wearing a lace shoulder wrap that covered the upper part of their dress.

Alex had spent the better part of the morning being prepared for her big moment. The hair and the makeup were flawless and then it was time to don the dress. She was gorgeous and had a glow about her that showed that all was right in her world.

Gail helped with the finishing touches and whispered in Alex's ear. "It is time to make some memories to last a lifetime."

Alex took Gail by the hand. "Thank you for all that your family has done." She looked as if she was going to cry.

Gail handed her a tissue. "You don't want runs in your makeup now. Save those tears until after the pictures have been taken." She rubbed Alex's hand. "Mrs. Tennant is trying to get the wedding party in place so I had better go." Gail dabbed a tear of her own. "Chad is one lucky young man."

Mrs. Tennant came up to Gail. "Mrs. Rollins. If you would be so kind to join the others we can have us a wedding."

"I'm on my way." Gail gave a parting wink and smile to the bride.

The bridal party took its place at the front of the church. Gail looked to where Alex would make her grand entrance and then checked out the crowd to see how many people she knew. It was hard to miss *The Angels of Mercy* as they beamed with pride while giving orders and directions like traffic cops. She saw a lot of Alex and Vicki's friends who were also her son's friends who had helped Jason prevent a lot of food from going stale.

Gail looked over at the groom's side of the hall and it was hard to keep her emotions in check when she saw B.S. Crappo sitting next to his wife. How did a man like that deserve such a nice looking wife? Next to them sat Jack and his wife. Gail knew that she really should be nicer to Jack than she was, after all Wade and Jack were friends. Why they were such good friends was still a mystery to her, but life is full of mysteries. Next to Jack sat an older couple who she determined must be Jack's grandparents. The physical resemblance was uncanny, except one of them had more wrinkles, and the other one had more hair. She never recognized anyone else from that side of the hall. She glanced at the front row and looked at the groom's parents. She found it hard to believe that someone that nice could even be remotely related to the Crappo's. Her gaze fell on the lady seated next to Chad's parents. She seemed unusually quiet and distant during this time of celebration. She was somber and looked as if this wedding was the last place on earth that she wanted to be.

Once again Gail glanced towards where Alex would make her grand entrance to be escorted down the aisle by the father who had abandoned his family. Gail thought about the man and tried to figure out why she had pushed for Alex to include him in her special day? Wade was perfectly willing to give her away but even he thought that it would be best to try and include the man, if for no other reason than to let him know what a wonderful daughter and family he had walked away from.

When the wedding march began to play it was time for Gail to focus on the task at hand. The young flower girls came down the aisle dropping rose petals for the bride to walk on. The flower girls were followed by the young ring bearer with the rings on a small satin pillow. Next was the moment Gail had waited for, Alex and her father came into view and started to move forward down the aisle. She was stunning in her wedding dress. The dress was absolutely beautiful but it was outclassed by the glow in Alex's eyes. She was radiant – a testament that all was right in her world.

The wedding march ended and the father released his grip on Alex's hand as he turned her over to Chad, the luckiest man in the room. The happy couple walked together to stand in front of the pastor who asked the guests to be seated before he began the ceremony.

"Dearly beloved we are gathered here today in the presence of God and these witnesses to join this couple, Alexandria Dawn Timpson and Chad Austin Hill, in holy matrimony." He paused and smiled at the couple in front of him. "If there are any here who think that this union should not take place let them speak now or forever hold their piece."

During the pause Gail detected motion from the corner of her eye and thought that B.S. Crappo was going to speak. Nothing happened as he settled back in his chair and sat quietly.

The pastor took a few moments and gave the couple some advice on marriage before he continued. "Do you Alexandria Dawn Timpson; take this man Chad Austin Hill to be your lawfully wedded husband to love and to hold for better or for worse, in sickness and in health, for richer or for poorer, as long as you both shall live?"

Alexandria Dawn Timpson took a small breath and uttered the words. "I do."

The pastor turned to Chad. "Do you Chad Austin Hill; take Alexandria Dawn Timpson to be your lawfully wedded wife to love and to hold for better or for worse, in sickness and in health, for richer or for poorer, as long as you both shall live?"

Chad Austin Hill took a deep breath as he stood silent looking into Alexandria's eyes but never said a word for the longest time. Tears rolled down his face when he said the words. "I do."

The couple exchanged their vows and then exchanged rings.

When the vows were finished the invitation to kiss the bride was issued and promptly accepted. The pastor had the couple turn to face the gathered guests and presented them as Mr. and Mrs. Chad Hill.

It was a special moment. Gail was happy for Alex and Chad but was at a loss to explain why she was being so emotional. She used as many, if not more tissues than the bride's mother to wipe away the tears.

The photographer was fantastic and really earned his keep as the bridal party and families were busy for most of the afternoon. By the time the reception was due to begin Gail was wishing that she had taken more time to sit instead of checking up on *The Angels of Mercy* and how things were progressing. Her feet were tired and beginning to swell. As she sat rubbing her feet Amber sat down beside her and asked, "Mommy, when are we supposed to do the bridesmaid dance?"

This innocent question intrigued Gail. "Who told you that the bridesmaids had to dance?"

"Jason did. He showed me videos of the dance after Alex asked me to be her bridesmaids so that I could practice."

Gail could see the look of accomplishment in Amber's eyes. "Jason did that for you?"

"Yes he did. Would you like to see the dance?"

Gail was curious as to what her son was up to. "I would love to see the dance."

Amber found a paper cup and stood on a table with the cup held above her head. She then proceeded to move her feet like a drunken chicken and almost fell off of the table. "Do you like my dance?"

Gail could only imagine what kind of videos Jason had selected but the title *Bridesmaids Gone Wild* came to mind. "You did a wonderful job. Is that why the cushions from my couch were always on the floor in the living room?"

"Yes, the floor hurt too much when I fell off of the table so I put the cushions on the floor to land on." Amber instinctively rubbed her butt where she had landed many times.

Gail looked at Amber with pride. "Why didn't you ask me to help you learn the dance?"

"Jason told me to not tell you and that I should surprise you when I had learned the dance."

Gail wanted to have a few words with Jason and have him tell Amber it was a joke but at the same time she didn't want to disappoint Amber after all of the effort she had put in learning the dance. Gail had to put an end to the madness before Amber hurt herself. "Did you learn the dance for Alex's wedding or for Amanda's?"

"Both."

Gail leaned close to Amber. "I don't think that Mrs. Tennant was planning on having that dance during the reception but I can ask her if you can do it."

Amber thought about the offer a few moments. "That's okay mom. The tables are much higher than at home and there are no cushions to land on. If they don't need me to dance then I won't do the dance."

Gail smiled. "I'm sure that will be just fine. Maybe for Amanda and Dale's wedding you and Jason can both do the dance together?"

The church hall was hub of activity as Mrs. Tennant, Gloria and Martha were making sure that people were in their places and things were being done the way they had planned. The food tables were stocked with Martha's dessert, glasses of water and glasses of a punch that Martha had decided to add at the last minute because water wasn't exciting.

The guests arriving at the reception were greeted with a slideshow playing in the foyer with pictures of the bride and groom growing up. The slide show was very well done and Gail wanted to see it in its entirety. Especially the pictures of Alex which reminded Gail of those tender moments they had shared in the hospital and since they were reunited.

Mrs. Tennant interrupted Gail's viewing of the slideshow when she came up and stood beside her. "Mrs. Rollins. May I ask why you are being so difficult today?"

Gail was surprised by this comment. "How am I being difficult?"

"You are being difficult by not following my directions."

"When have I not followed your directions today?"

Mrs. Tennant reverted to her official tone of voice. "Like right now. I called for the receiving line to gather and you walked away and came over here."

Gail wanted to watch the end of the slide show but didn't want to cause a scene. She took her place in the line next to Alex and waited for the groom's side to fill the line before they could start receiving guests. Gail leaned close to Alex. "Did you put Mrs. Tennant in charge of the line up as well?"

Alex smiled. "No but she thinks that she is in charge." Alex snickered. "Did she give you detention for being in the hall without permission?"

Gail was unable to respond as the first people started to come through the line. Gail looked over to the dessert table to see if Vicki's desserts had made it on display. It looked as if Martha's desserts were still the only ones there. She leaned to Vicki. "Did your father make it here with the desserts?"

"I don't know but I will check." Vicki stepped out of the line and placed a call. She returned a few moments later and took her place beside Gail. "My father never answered his phone."

Gail wanted to continue her conversation but stopped when she had a guest in front of her.

The somber lady who had sat beside Chad's parents during the wedding ceremony was standing before her. She wasn't very talkative and waited for her turn to stand in front of Alex. The lady took her place in front of Alex and started to cry as she exclaimed how beautiful a bride Alex was. Then she moved to Chad to congratulate him with a big tearful hug and a sloppy kiss on the cheek.

As the lady moved along the line Chad leaned over to Gail. "She is one of my mom's sisters. She lost her daughter when the girl was very young so she gets emotional at events like this."

Gail watched Chad's aunt make her way from the reception line, stop for some food and drink, and then sit at the table with B.S. Crappo and his wife. Gail watched the woman and thought to herself. "That poor unfortunate soul, it's bad enough to lose a child, but being related to the Crappo family as well must be a fate worse than death."

The line moved at a steady pace but it still seemed to go on forever. Gail could feel her feet swelling as she stood. Wade brought a tray of desserts and some glasses of water for the girls in the receiving line. "Is there anything else I can get you?"

"Can you bring us some punch?" Gail asked.

"I'd rather not. When you drink the punch after eating the dessert it leaves a medicinal taste in your mouth." Wade shivered and pretended to gag. "Water is better for you. Trust me on this."

Gail laughed at Wade's antics. "It can't be that bad."

"Worse." Wade scraped the top of his tongue with his teeth and wrinkled his nose.

Gail greeted a few more guests and turned back to Wade. "Did Angelo get here with the leftovers?"

Wade gave Gail a puzzled look. "Angelo is bringing leftovers to the wedding?"

Gail laughed as she realised that she had kept that small detail from Wade. "Leftover is our code word for the dessert Vicki made for the reception?"

Wade scratched his head. "I don't understand. All I see on the table are the desserts Martha made."

She gave has hand a squeeze and released her grip. "Don't worry about it. I will get one of the good desserts when we are done here. In the meantime tell Jason to stop eating these ones."

Wade winked at Gail. "That shouldn't be a problem. Jason just borrowed some money and went to the burger joint around the corner."

"And did you give him enough to buy something for all of us?" Gail asked.

Wade looked sheepish before he left. "No just enough to get something for him and something for me to get rid of the medicinal taste from the desserts."

Gail watched Wade make his way to the door and sighed. She whispered to Vicki. "The least he could have done was to take these desserts with him."

A few minutes later Gail was speaking with Erin Crappo while her husband Jack stopped to speak with Amber. They stopped talking and listened to what Jack was saying to Amber.

Jack leaned down to Amber. "Young lady you are even lovelier in person. The pictures that your dad keeps on his desk do not do you justice.

Amber smiled. "Thank you."

Jack joined Erin where he was greeted by Gail. "Jack it is so nice to see you and Erin again. It has been a while."

"Yes it has. We need to do something to correct that."

Erin took Jack by the hand. "This has been a nice day. I'm so glad that you and Wade could help share the joy of this young couple. It means a lot to us."

"It means a lot to us as well. They are special kids."

Gail surveyed the line and gulped. In a few moments she was going to be face to face with the man she despised more than anyone else in the world, and she was going to have to be gracious and civil. Before that meeting was going to happen Gail noticed that the somber lady was in front of them coming through the line a second time. Only this time she was more animated than the time before. Gail held out her hand and took the lady by the hand. "I'm pleased to meet you again."

The lady was no more talkative than before as she waited her turn with Alex. This time instead of crying he took Alex by the hand a few moments and told her how lovely she was before she moved on to Chad where the encounter was just a brief handshake as she moved on for another dessert and some punch.

Now was the moment of truth for Gail as she was about to come face to face with B.S. Crappo and his wife. She had mixed emotions as they met because part of her wanted to greet this wonderful lady with a hug, while the other part wanted to sock her husband in the nose. Gail smiled graciously. "Mr. and Mrs. Crappo, I'm so glad that you were able to attend the wedding and share in Alex and Chad's joy."

Mrs Crappo carried the conversation while her husband stood behind her and kept an awkward silence. "Chad has found a lovely girl."

Gail responded. "And Alex has found a wonderful young man."

Gail looked at B.S. Crappo and had a few choice remarks that stayed in the holster as she couldn't help but think that the wife had no idea what pain her husband had brought into her life. She forced a smile. "We really should get together more often. It's a shame that we never seem to be able to attend the same functions at the country club."

"No kidding. Wade and Jack are such good friends. We should make more of an effort to get together."

In spite of the disdain she held for the man in front of her, Gail kept her composure. With each word the wife said, BS Crappo looked more and more uncomfortable. It was fun watching the big bad lawyer squirm. "We will just have to make more of an effort to make that happen. It would be fun to spend time together." As Mrs.Crappo turned her attention to Alex, Gail shot a glare at BS Crappo that would have been mistaken by none who had seen it.

A few people later Gail was speaking to Jack's Grandfather and Grandmother. It was a pleasant encounter which made Gail wonder how their son could have turned out to be such a jerk.

One of the last guests through the reception line had also been one of the first through the line as the somber lady came through for a third time, only this time she was upbeat and bubbly; a mood that was more fitting for the occasion. When she arrived at Alex she told her how lovely she looked but this time she gave Alex a hug that was long enough to be uncomfortable, while her greeting for Chad could have set a record for brevity.

When the reception line was over Gail could hardly wait to sit down and remove the shoes from her feet. Vicki sat down beside her and rubbed her own feet as well as she commented on the people they had greeted in the line. "That was an adventure with how many times that lady kept coming through the line and how differently she acted each time."

Gail smiled. "She was different."

Vicki laughed. "She was at that." Vicki paused. "You don't think that her reason for so many trips through the line was just to get more desserts and glasses of punch do you? She had a lot of them."

Gail placed her shoes under her chair and started to rub her other foot. "Maybe the reason she came through the line so many times was that she never knew that she could just go back to the table for seconds." Gail placed her feet on the floor and compared them to see just how badly swollen they were. She looked at Vicki. "Did you notice how each time through the line she acted more alive than the time before?"

Vicki nodded. "And the only thing that changed was the amount of dessert she had to eat and all those glasses of punch she had to drink." Vicki looked around the hall. "Maybe Martha has discovered a cure for depression with her food." She then changed the subject. "Who were those people that you were polite to but sounded like you don't like?"

"Did I really sound like I don't like them?"

"Not to worry Mrs. Rollins, only people who know you might have noticed." Vicki rubbed her feet again. "Did you ever see any of my desserts make it to the table?"

"I can't say that I did but if they had made it to the table I am sure that Jason would have found them."

They shared a laugh as they watched Martha bring several plates of her dessert to Alex and Chad with some glasses of punch as she encouraged them to eat.

Vicki put her shoes back onto her feet. "I should try to call my father again. The reception is almost over." Vicki dialed a number and nodded her head as she listened to the voice on the phone. She ended the call and turned to Gail. "It seems that dad did come past with the food but was told in no uncertain terms that this wedding deserved better food than leftovers from another party."

Gail looked at Vicki. "And what happened?"

"Mrs. Tennant and Martha put the run on him." Vicki smiled. "So how many trays of leftovers would you like delivered to your home?"

Gail watched Chad and Alex politely eat the desserts as Martha watched them. "That all depends on who made them."

There was a short program planned for before the dance which included some musical numbers by family and friends, followed by a brief slide show with commentary of the happy couple growing up. The last slide to be shown was that of a lovely beach on a tropical island at sunset. While the picture of the beautiful pristine beach with the receding tide remained on the screen, Jack Crappo added one final commentary. "This picture of the beach at sunset is definitely beautiful to look at but can anyone tell me what is missing from the picture?" There was silence in the hall until Jack continued speaking. "What I find missing from this picture is footprints in the sand. Footprints made by two very special people who we all know and love." Jack turned to Chad and Alex. "This needs to be corrected. As a gift to you, courtesy of your families and friends, these beaches will soon be covered with your foot prints during your honeymoon," Jack paused and smiled. "That is if you actually make it to the beach."

Amber tugged on Gail's sleeve. "So this is when people learn where they go on their honeymoon?"

"This is when Alex and Chad learned where they are going."

Jack handed an envelope to Chad. "We brought your travelling clothes along with your packed suitcases." Jack signaled for the music to start. "You have time for a short first dance and then we need to get you to the airport."

The first dance was a blur and soon the newlyweds were on their way for a tropical honeymoon.

CHAPTER SIXTEEN

Wade scratched at the stains on the front of his shirt. "I sure hope that the stain from Martha's dessert will come out of my shirt and tie." He scratched a few more times before he tossed the shirt into the laundry basket. "At least the punch never burned a hole in the fabric. That is one of my best dress shirts."

Gail removed her dress and placed it on a hanger. She hung the dress in her closet and turned to Wade. "Are you sure that the stain is from the dessert and not from the grease burger with fries that Jason got for you from the hamburger joint?"

Wade looked at Gail. "Are you still upset that Jason never got a hamburger for you and Amber?"

Gail let down her hair and ran her fingers through it to remove the braids. "The hamburger didn't look that appetising but a strawberry milkshake would have been nice."

Wade burped. "The milkshake wasn't that good either, but it did help cover the medicinal taste from Martha's punch."

"You had a milkshake too?" Gail stopped brushing her hair and pointed the hair brush at Wade. "Did Jason have to go back for the milkshake or did he buy it when he bought the burger and fries?"

Wade forced a small burp. "Boy that burger is still sitting heavy." Wade forced another small burp and held his stomach. "You should be thanking me for sparing you from the experience."

Gail watched Wade rummage through his dresser. "Jason went back to the hamburger joint a second time for the milkshakes didn't he."

Wade turned towards Gail as he retrieved his pyjamas from under his pillow. "You and Amber were better off just drinking water. My stomach is rebelling for how I mistreated it tonight and I bet if you check in on Jason he is feeling the same way as I am."

Gail shook her head as she tried to ignore the last comment. She sat on the edge of the bed and rubbed her feet with anti inflammatory cream. "Standing in wedding lines is a young person job. My feet are killing me."

Wade reached over and tickled the bottom of Gail's foot. "Your feet may be killing you but you and I both know that you wouldn't have missed being Alex's Matron of Honor."

Gail pulled her foot away from Wade and placed it on the floor. "True, I wouldn't have missed the experience of being a part of Alex's wedding – even though I had B.S. Crappo in my sights and had to be nice to him."

Wade smiled and a snicker slipped out. "You did a wonderful job keeping your inner thoughts to yourself."

Gail didn't know what to make of Wade's snicker as he spoke about her encounter. "Did I at least look and sound sincere when I acted like I enjoyed speaking to them?"

Wade pick up Gail's hairbrush from the makeup table and held it to his mouth like a microphone. "And the Oscar for best actress in an awkward situation goes to Gail Rollins."

Gail hit him with a pillow. "I'm serious. Did I look sincere or do you think that they know that I don't like him by how I sounded?"

Wade returned the hairbrush to the table. "You had me fooled. That is until you gave Jack's father the Death Stare."

"You saw that?"

"Yes I saw it but only because I was watching you to see what I might have to apologise for."

Gail tried to hit him with the pillow. "Did you see me do anything else you might have to apologise for?"

Wade blocked the hit and placed the pillow on the bed. "No, after Jack and his family had gone through the line without incident I went with Jason for some real food."

Gail shook her head. "But you didn't get food for your wife and daughter."

Wade forced another small burp and pressed against his stomach as it gurgled loud enough to be heard. "I thought of you when I realized that nothing we bought from the burger place would have been healthy enough for you to serve at home. So I was thinking of you." The stomach gurgled again.

Gail hit Wade with the other pillow. "Thanks a lot." She placed the pillow on the bed. "Did you see how many times Chad's aunt came through the line?"

"Three times that I counted but I wasn't there for the entire time. How many times did she come through?"

"Three, but did you notice how each time she went through the line she became more animated and emotional?"

"Yes I did notice a change in her behavior." Wade went into the bathroom for an antacid and chewed two tablets before he returned to the bedroom.

"So what do you think caused the change in her behavior?"

Wade pulled down the sheets and was ready to climb into bed. "I'm not sure what caused the change in her behavior; but I know if I had consumed that much of Martha's punch and dessert I would act strange if I wasn't in the hospital to have my stomach pumped."

Gail watched Wade pull the covers over him. "Seriously, what do you think caused the change?"

Wade yawned. "I heard some people think that it may have been the combination of the punch and dessert, it does taste like medicine when consumed together."

"You mean that people think that the combination of the dessert and punch affected her in a good way, almost like an awakening?"

"Like a what?" Wade asked as he folded his pillow to prop up his head.

Gail pulled down her covers and climbed into bed. "An awakening, like what happened in the movie where mental patients came out of their coma's for a short time with a new drug therapy."

"Where did that come from?"

Gail folded her pillow to prop up her head as she rolled to face Wade. "Martha is excited to think that someone wanted her recipes for the punch and dessert because they think the food might have had something to do with the ladies change in behavior."

"That food definitely changed my behavior; but like I said; if I had as much of that food to eat as she did I would be in the hospital getting my stomach pumped."

"Be nice, Martha only wanted to help with the wedding and did the best she could."

"I suppose that she did." Wade rolled over in discomfort as his stomach gurgled again. "I am sure glad that I never ate any more of Martha's offerings than I did."

Gail went thoughtful as she waited for Wade to stop rolling around in discomfort. "What if the food Martha made had nothing to do with the change in the ladies behavior?"

"Then we might have a mystery on our hands." Wade reached for the light switch and turned out the lights.

As she lay in the dark waiting for sleep to come Gail nudged Wade. "What if something else did happen to cause the change in her behavior?"

Wade turned the light back on but before he could say anything Jason came into the room scratching his neck and stomach.

"Mom did you use that laundry soap on my clothes that makes me itch?" Jason started to scratch his legs and rubbed his back against the corner of the wall."It sure feels like you did."

"No I got rid of that soap." Gail climbed out of bed and went into her bathroom. She returned and handed Jason some antihistamines. "Take two of these and see if that helps while I run you a bath."

CHAPTER SEVENTEEN

Things had been quiet around the Rollins residence since the wedding. Alex and Chad were on their honeymoon and supposed to return home from their honeymoon today but Gail wasn't expecting a visit – after all what newlywed wants company on their honeymoon?

Gail placed a load of laundry into the washing machine and hesitated before adding the soap and starting the cycle. Normally she would wait for a larger load but not today. Jason had asked her to wash his prized lucky basketball socks and she wasn't going to miss this opportunity to return the crusty socks into a sweet smelling pliable piece of clothing. When he had asked her to wash them the last time she had waited for a larger load of laundry and Jason took the socks before they were washed. That was over a month of basketball ago. She added the soap and hit the start button. As she watched the clothes tumble she had a passing thought – I hope the rest of the clothes don't pick up the smell.

She was in the kitchen placing Jason's' breakfast dishes into the dishwasher when the door bell sounded. Gail waited to see if her children were going to answer the door and when they didn't she answered the door herself. Gail was both surprised and excited to find Alex and Chad on her doorstep.

"Please come in." Gail greeted them with a hug before she offered to take their jackets and showed them to the living room.

Amber entered the living room and rushed to Alex. She wrapped her arms around Alex's legs and asked, "How was your honeymoon?"

Alex gave Amber a hug and kissed her cheek. "It was wonderful."

Amber then extended a hand to Chad for him to shake.

Chad shook her hand. "No hugs for me?"

Amber placed her hands on her hips. "I hardly know you." She turned to Gail who was having difficulty keeping a straight face. "Mommy, can I go over to Suzie's house and play?"

Gail had wanted to say no but because she wanted to have a peaceful visit with Alex and Chad said yes. Before giving permission Gail made sure that Amber was aware of her wishes. "Do you promise not to ask about the window sticker on the back of their van?"

Amber lowered her head. "Okay."

"Good, now run along."

When Amber was out of the house Chad asked, "What is so special about the window sticker?"

Gail wanted to talk about the honeymoon more than the sticker but she answered the question. "The sticker is the one representing Suzie's father and part, no, almost all of the body is missing and it bothers Amber that the sticker isn't being fixed."

"Why don't they fix it?"

Gail sighed. "Once their divorce is final the rest of the sticker will be removed."

Chad rubbed his chin. "I see."

Gail turned to Alex. "So was your honeymoon everything you expected it would be?"

Alex glanced at Chad. "It was everything we expected and more."

"What happened that you weren't expecting?"

Alex placed her hand on top of Chad's hand. "During our flight Chad started getting very itchy and started to get a rash all over his body."

"Were the flight attendants able to help?"

Alex smiled. "Nothing they had on board helped relieve the symptoms so they called ahead to have medical assistance waiting for Chad when we landed."

Gail's interest was piqued. "What did they determine to be the problem?"

Chad rubbed his arms and sighed. "They weren't able to determine what was happening so they put me in quarantine without any contact with Alex for two days until it cleared up."

"That's interesting." Gail smiled as she wondered how they handled the interruption to their togetherness.

"What is interesting?" Alex asked as she watched Gail smile grow.

Gail was able to keep her composure as she spoke. "Jason and several other guests started to itch and develop a rash after you left the reception. Jason's symptoms lasted about two days."

When Gail said the word rash Chad rubbed his arms again. "What do you think caused the rash?"

Gail started to laugh. "We called it Martha's Dessertitis."

Alex gasped. "Do you really think the dessert caused it?"

"Wade had an itch after the reception but it wasn't as severe as Jason's. They both had the dessert and punch but Jason ate a lot more than Wade did." Gail smiled. "Jason broke out after the reception with the same symptoms. We think it was an allergic reaction to the combination of the dessert and the punch. How much did you eat?"

Chad thought a moment. "I had the three pieces of the dessert that Martha made us eat and two glasses of punch."

Alex looked at Gail. "So why didn't the dessert affect me like it did Chad?"

"You drank water after only taking the small sip of punch." Gail rubbed her hands and smiled. "So Alex what did you do alone in Hawaii for two days while Chad was in quarantine?"

"Not much. I was worried about Chad so I never did anything except sit on the beach in front of the hotel."

"You do have a lovely tan." Gail turned to Chad. "So after they let you go were you able to continue your honeymoon as if nothing happened?"

Chad placed a hand in front of his mouth to hide a grin as he winked at Alex. "More or less."

"So what did you do?"

Alex played with Chad's fingers. "We went to a beach with another couple I had met at the hotel before Chad was released from quarantine." Alex started to chuckle. "It was a clothing optional beach so we opted to go au natural and Chad got sunburned where a person should never sunburn."

Chad shifted uncomfortably. "The sunburn was so bad that I blistered and needed medical attention."

Alex started to laugh hard enough that she had tears in her eyes. "We had to stay in the hotel room the following day and use room service because it hurt Chad to even wear his loose fitting swimsuit."

Gail knew that she was losing the battle to keep a straight face and it got even harder when Chad blushed enough to glow red over his new suntan. "Were you able to see much of the island while you were there?"

"We saw enough for me to know that I would like to go back again." Alex nudged Chad. "Only next time we will take sunscreen."

Chad returned the nudge. "I'm taking sun block."

Gail could feel joy for the happiness Chad and Alex had found and the joy they shared. "So the honeymoon was everything you could have hoped for – in spite of the unexpected memories."

"It was great and now we are back to reality." Alex lowered her head ever so slightly and for a brief moment her smile disappeared before she caught herself and smiled as she had before.

Gail picked up on the moment but was unsure if she should let it pass or say something. She remembered the card that Dale had sent and got it from the hallway shelf. "Dale sent this card but wondered if he should continue to call you Alex or if Alexandria is more appropriate now that you are a married woman?"

Alex paused. "I suppose that Alexandria would seem more appropriate but either will work."

Gail looked at Chad. "Is there any preference for you how we address your wife?"

Chad took Alex's hand. "Right about now either would be fine." He paused briefly. "Just do not call her Lexie."

That was not the answer Gail had expected. She hadn't heard that name since she and Alex were reunited. "I would never consider calling her Lexie, but out of curiosity why is the name Lexie a problem?"

Chad shook his head. "Lexie is the name of the daughter that Aunt Janice lost."

Gail was glad Amber wasn't here to ask questions, heaven knows Gail now had enough of her own questions to ask. "So why is the name Lexie now a cause for concern?"

Chad took a deep breath and slowly allowed the air to escape his pursed lips. "Aunt Janice is convinced that Alex is the daughter she had to give up for adoption and is telling everyone who will listen to her that Alex is her Lexie."

Gail could see why this development could be cause for concern. "Does she have any proof that Alex could be Lexie?"

Chad bit at his lower lip. "She has all of Lexie's baby pictures and the last pictures she has match the earliest pictures we used for Alex in the slide show at the reception."

Gail was beginning to piece things together as to why the demeanor of this woman had changed during the reception. Being separated from Alex at the hospital had been an emotional event for Gail that affected her to where Alex had been continually on her mind. Gail could only imagine how emotional she would become and how she would react to potentially finding the child she had been forced to give up for adoption, especially if the child she found could actually be hers. "So it wasn't Martha's dessert and punch that brought about the change in Janice."

Chad spoke up. "No, it would seem that the only thing the punch did for Aunt Janice was give her a bad rash and an itch." He put his arm around Alex. "The change came because of the slideshow. Every time Janice watched the slideshow she became more convinced that she had found her long lost daughter. It had nothing to do with us being married and especially not because of the food."

Gail sat silent as the reality of the situation came to her. "So if Janice is correct and Alex is her daughter – then the two of you are first cousins."

Chad put his arm around Alex and gave a squeeze. "That is what people are saying."

Gail was unsure what to say as she watched the frustration start to show on the faces of this lovely couple. Before being swept up in the apparent helplessness of the situation Gail had a thought come to her. "Alex when your current mother fell ill you had said that you had two mothers before her. So is it possible that Janice is mother number two and not your birthmother?"

Alex lowered her eyes. "I asked that same question."

The suspense was killing Gail. "And what was the answer?"

Alex held a tissue to her nose as she sniffled. "I was told that there is no other mother before Janice."

"Then why would they tell you that you had been adopted? It just doesn't make any sense."

Chad took Alex by the hand and played his fingers between hers. "You need to know Janice's ex-husband to understand the situation." Chad paused. "I never knew the man very well but I was told that he never wanted children and liked his money and drinking more than he liked children. So whenever Lexie did something he didn't approve of he would say that she was adopted because no kid of his would do something that stupid."

Gail was appalled to think that a mother would allow that behavior to happen. "Why didn't Janice say something?"

"It was easier and safer not to argue with him because when he had been drinking he would become violent. It seems that Janice said nothing and just played along to keep the peace."Chad looked at Gail with a peaceful expression. "The accident that put Lexie in the hospital was a blessing in disguise."

Gail could scarcely believe the story being told. "So how is it that you feel that the car accident was a blessing in disguise?"

Chad slowly rubbed the back of Alex's neck. "The car accident was a blessing in disguise because Alex met you in the hospital." Chad placed his arm around Alex's shoulder and held her close to him. "Plus because of the circumstances with Janice's husband and the things he was involved with that put his family at risk; Alex was able to be adopted into a loving family who could raise her in a safe environment."

Gail wiped a tear from her eye and took Alex by the hand. "Had I known, I would have adopted you the first moment we met in the hospital."

Alex placed her hand on Gail's hand and gave a gentle squeeze. "I believe that you would have."

Gail looked at Chad. "What does your family think about Janice's claim?"

Chad closed his eyes and turned his head to the side. "Uncle Jack's father told us that unless proven otherwise; we must assume that Aunt Janice is Alex's mother."

Alex started to sob. "Jack's father even served us with papers."

Seeing the pain this situation was causing these two young people Gail could feel her dislike for B.S Crappo grow even larger than usual. "What papers did he serve you with?"

Neither one of the couple could speak so Chad pulled a paper from his pocket and handed it to Gail to read. Gail looked at the paper in disbelief and wanted to give Chad and Alex a hug and tell them that everything was going to be alright. She read the paper a few times hoping that what she read was nothing more than a cruel ill timed practical joke. *Chad and Alexandria. The possibility exists that Janice is Alex's mother and the two of you are first cousins. Cease and desist in all activities related to consummating your nuptials. If you fail to stop you will be breaking the law.* ***This marriage may need to be annulled.***

CHAPTER EIGHTEEN

Dale sat behind the desk of what he referred to as his temporary assignment from hell. Not because it was a bad assignment but more because it was keeping him away from Amanda. Being separated from Amanda was bad enough but it was killing him to think of Adam being with her. He called Amanda at every opportunity just to hear her voice and give him a chance to tell her that he loved her, but each time something inside kept him from declaring his love for her over the phone.

He booked the time off and planned to visit Amanda as his birthday present to himself. The purpose for the visit was to get down on one knee and propose to the girl of his dreams as he put a ring on her finger.

The taxi arrived and Dale was about to close the door behind him when the phone rang. He debated if he should answer it or just let it ring. He returned to answer the phone – just in case it was Amanda.

"Hello?" Dale was full of optimism until he heard the deep voice on the other end.

"Dale I need to see you in my office at once."

Dale sighed, the last person he wanted to speak with right now was his supervisor and for a split second considered hanging up on him, but thought better of it. "Is it urgent? I am on my way to the airport to start my vacation."

"Yes it is urgent. Be in my office in ten minutes and bring your luggage."

Dale listened to the dial tone sounding in his ear and muttered a few select words in frustration that when he was younger, had his mother heard them, would have earned him a free tasting of a soap bar lollipop. Dale hung up the phone and muttered. "Happy Birthday to me...not!" Dale was at the office in less than ten minutes and presented himself to the receptionist who motioned for him to enter.

He set his luggage on the floor outside of the office door and knocked. "You wanted to see me sir?"

"Yes, please take a seat and I will be right with you."

Dale took a seat and waited for the last piece of paper to be signed. He looked at his watch and knew that if all went well he could still catch his flight. He was curious for the reason he would be called in when he had been approved for his time away. He only had a few moments to wonder before it was his turn.

"Dale I need you to attend a wedding that I was supposed to attend with my wife until she became ill."

Dale heard those words; *attend a wedding*, and wanted to scream. Why should the wedded bliss of others always come before his? He remained calm as he listened to the details. In different circumstances or even a different weekend he would have been ecstatic to attend this wedding; he knew the bride and loved the destination. But this weekend was not a good weekend because he had already made plans. Most importantly he planned to ensure his future happiness by proposing to Amanda.

A package was placed on the desk in front of Dale. "Here are your tickets and itinerary. You need to be at the airport in an hour."

Dale looked at the tickets and couldn't believe his eyes. The trip had a five hour layover at his original destination so he would still be able to see Amanda. The proposal would be a day earlier than planned but he was okay with that. He was going to see Amanda. Dale's mood changed and he was now able to look at his supervisor with a sincere smile. "I will be happy to do this for you."

Dale boarded the plane and thought of how surprised Amanda would be to see him. He questioned the wisdom of not telling Amanda his plans for the weekend but he wanted to surprise her so he never gave it a second thought. Soon he would be reunited with Amanda - even if it was only for a few hours.

The plane landed but still had to wait on the tarmac for the better part of an hour before reaching the terminal. Dale was the first passenger to arrive at the baggage area and was noticeably annoyed as he waited for the baggage to arrive. When the baggage carrousel jammed for the third time he was ready to climb up the chute to find his bag. Dale knew that should he climb the chute his actions would be considered irrational but that was the least of his concerns.

He waited impatiently as the bags were slid down the chute and onto the carrousel by hand. Twenty three minutes later he claimed his bag and caught a taxi to his apartment. Dale dropped his bags just inside the front door and went into his bedroom to get the ring from his nightstand drawer. Dale bought a small bouquet of flowers from the vendor on the corner and then made the short walk to the office in record time. As he walked he rehearsed in his mind how he was going to propose to Amanda. Dale touched his pocket to confirm that he still had the ring as he entered the familiar confines of the office. He went straight to Amanda's desk prepared to present her the flowers and the ring as he dropped to one knee with a declaration of his love for her. His heart dropped when he reached the desk and found it organized the way it always was before Amanda left for the day – and no Amanda.

He looked towards his office and found it dark with the door closed. He was disappointed that he wouldn't even be able see what this Adam character looked like and give him a piece of his mind for messing with him. Dale drew a deep breath then sighed. Just then there was a noise behind him and he turned to see a friendly face. "Janet, do you know where Amanda is?"

Janet greeted Dale with a hug. "What a pleasant surprise to see you. Are here to stay?"

"Not this time but I am hoping to be here to stay in a few weeks if all goes well. Today I'm on my way to another assignment. I had a layover so I wanted to stop in and spend some time with Amanda. Do you know where she is?"

Ashley came into the room and came over to greet Dale. "It's nice to see you stranger." She gave him a small hug. "Let me put those flowers in some water for you. Amanda will be so disappointed that she missed you."

Dale handed Ashley the flowers. "Where is Amanda?"

Ashley and Janet looked at each other in an awkward silence. "She isn't here."

Dale was getting an uneasy feeling. "I can see that. Where is she?"

Ashley licked her lips. "Amanda went away with Adam for the weekend." She cringed slightly. "But they will be back on Monday."

Dale took a deep breath and tried not to show his disappointment but was certain that he had failed to hide it. "Do you know where they went?"

"I wish that I had an answer for you." Ashley smelled the flowers. "Amanda never told us where they were going because Adam was keeping the destination a surprise from her."

"How could it be a surprise when Amanda books all of the flights in the office?"

"Not this time. Adam booked everything. He even packed a bag for her so that she wouldn't know where they might be going."

"He packed her bag for her?" Dale could feel his dislike for Adam grow exponentially as he had visions of Amanda opening a suitcase and finding pyjamas that could only keep her warm in a heat wave. "What do you think his intentions are?"

"Did you know that Adam and Amanda have started dating?" Janet received a sharp nudge to the ribs from Ashley.

Ashley spoke up. "They are not dating. They just go out a lot."

Dale looked at Janet. "What makes you think that they are dating?" Dale began to wonder why Amanda had failed to share that information with him during their numerous conversations. "How long has this been going on?"

"They started going out on her birthday." Janet received another nudge but this time a bit harder.

Dale tried to remain calm. "So do you think that Amanda likes him?

Ashley sighed as she looked at Dale. "Not as much as much as Adam seems to like her."

"All of this would be a non issue if you would have already proposed to Amanda." Janet received another nudge to the ribs and looked annoyed.

Dale removed the ring box from his pocket and showed the ring to the girls." Dale wiped at a small tear. "I have been trying to propose to Amanda in person since Consuela's wedding but work has gotten in my way." He wiped at another tear. "How could I have been so stupid and not let her know how I feel about her before now?"

Ashley put an arm around Dale. "She knows how you feel."

CHAPTER NINETEEN

*D*ale had a heavy heart as he made his way to the airport to catch his flight. He was not happy with the prospects of once again being a wedding guest at another wedding he never wanted any part of. Dale sat in the airport waiting for the flight and became even more miserable as he recalled the last conversation he had with Adam on Amanda's birthday. Even then Adam had been taunting Dale about his intentions to propose to Amanda before being cut off in mid sentence. Dale clenched his fist in frustration because he still didn't know if the call was dropped or if Adam had deliberately hung up on him. Either way, Adam had to be dealt with. Dale had no distractions and was soon fantasizing about the many undiplomatic things he wanted to do to Adam when they met.

Once the short flight had landed and Dale had cleared customs he walked outside of the airport and took the first cab he found to his hotel. The bags were taken to his room and he tipped the bell hop. Dale went to the window and admired the view. The tall ships in the harbour were still as majestic as he remembered them as they mingled with the numerous yachts in the harbour. There were more yachts than normal, most likely because of the wedding.

In the distance he saw the presidential palace on top of a hill overlooking the massive expanse of sandy beaches that stretched in either direction as far as the eye could see. All of the beaches were filled with people enjoying a perfect day in the sun; Dale couldn't help but notice the large number of happy couples enjoying each other's company. His gaze moved closer to town until he was looking at the clock tower in the town square surrounded by people going about their business. It was getting late and the sun was setting in the western sky and looked as if it was going into the sea when Dale turned away from the window and unpacked his suitcase. He took special care as he hung up his suit to allow the wrinkles to relax before he wore it to the wedding.

Amanda lay in the large comfortable bed and rubbed her hand over the silk sheets as she watched the sunlight slowly creep across the wall. She stretched her hands above her head and then rolled onto her side as she looked out of the window at the endless expanse of azure blue water. Amanda had no idea where in the world she was right now. The small executive jet that they boarded to start the trip had landed at an airport next to the harbour where the yacht that she was on had set sail from. Adam had definitely planned a weekend getaway that would be hard to match. The rhythmic drone of the yacht's powerful engines stopped and now the only movement she felt was the relaxing sensation of the yacht bobbing like a cork on the pond in her parents' back yard.

Amanda may not know where she was but she did know what day it was. Today was Dale's birthday. Amanda lay in bed surrounded by all this luxury and the potential for fun that this trip had to offer, but deep inside the desire of her heart was to hear Dale's voice and to wish him a happy birthday. Amanda took a deep breath and wiped her eyes as she remembered the promise she had made before her own birthday about moving on and was still unsure if that was a promise she wanted to keep.

Even though she had given serious thought about her future before she had made the promise, the yearning she felt in her heart made her question her decision. If Dale hadn't proposed to her by the end of his birthday was she really willing to move on and entertain the advances of other men? Amanda found herself thinking of Dale and how he might be spending his birthday but most of all she wished that she could talk to him and share the feelings in her heart. After all it would be wrong to walk away from Dale without giving him at least one more chance to make her the happiest girl in the world.

Amanda took some time to give serious consideration of what her future might look like if Dale was not part of the equation. At this time the future looked bleak since there were not a lot of suitable options in men for her to choose from; right now her pool of eligible suitors to replace Dale was a whopping list of one – Adam. While Adam was nice enough and she enjoyed being in the company of this handsome man, Amanda wasn't sure if he was a man she could commit to; or if he could truly commit to her. There was no denying that Amanda enjoyed being seen with Adam and the way the other girls looked at her when she was on his arm, but was that enough? Amanda was concerned that her attraction to Adam was more an infatuation with his physical appearance and the lifestyle he offered. Could a man like Adam make her heart feel the way it felt when she was with Dale?

Since allowing Adam to be part of her life in Dale's absence Amanda had experienced many things she had only dreamed of doing, if she had even considered doing them at all. She had been uncertain about saying yes to his invitation to join him and some friends for a week end of skydiving. The skydiving had been a wonderful experience once she got over the initial panic caused from the thought of jumping out of a perfectly fine airplane and plunging towards the earth. While Adam's friends that had joined them for the weekend seemed nice enough, they lived a different lifestyle and at no time during the weekend did she ever really feel that she fit in.

The weekend at a formula one race had been nice but in retrospect she had to admit that once again she had felt more like she was being tolerated by some of his other friends than accepted. Being allowed to drive a formula one car around the course had been a highlight for her even though she never pushed to see how fast she could make the car move. Amanda sighed, even though it had been nice to experience these things it seemed wrong that the fondest memories were about things she had done and not for any feelings she had for those she was with.

Now here she was on a beautiful yacht sailing on an ocean or maybe a sea going to who knows where with Adam. She could speculate where they were going and what the plans for the weekend were but what good would that do? One thing for certain was that this time she had none of Adam's friends with them to make her feel uncomfortable or feel like she was being tolerated. She had to admit that she enjoyed this lifestyle but at the same time she had to caution herself about falling for a lifestyle and all of the material goods over a relationship based on love. That being said, Adam and this lifestyle were definitely winning her over.

Still the way she felt when she was with Dale would make him hard to walk away from just because she had picked an arbitrary day to make a stand. Amanda had feelings for Dale that ran deep and she doubted that she would ever get over him should they part ways. Amanda sighed, and then there was Dale's family who accepted her and made her feel welcome to where she felt that she was part of their family. Dales' family were now her friends – really good friends.

Amanda acknowledged that one day she was going to have to make a decision and rubbed her face with her hands before she climbed out of bed. She stood at the window and looked at the vast expanse of water. She got dressed and as she reached for the door handle had a thought that made her hesitate. What if Adam were to propose to her this weekend, before she saw Dale again? She took a moment to follow the thought through since she had her suspicions that all of these weekends weren't just for her entertainment; there had to be a reason for him to put forth the effort and matrimony seemed to be the logical conclusion.

Amanda lightly bit her lip as she considered the potential situation and pondered how she would respond. If Adam were to propose marriage would she say no to this man who is showing interest in her and risk losing him while hoping for Dale to come through – or would she yes?

It was hard for Amanda to stop thinking of Dale and she was distracted as she climbed the steps onto the deck and stood next to the rail admiring the view of the island she had been unable to see from her cabin window. Not only were they anchored next to the island but they were anchored close to some other yachts. Her enjoyment of the moment lessened when she recognised Adam's friends on one of the yachts. As she stood there she remembered the disgust she had felt for this friend of Adam's who had taken liberties at the formula one weekend. Amanda had been offended when he came up behind her and placed his hand on her hip before he slid his hand down and grabbed her butt firmly and laughed while he declared it to be prime real estate. She had thought that she was over the incident but it seemed that she wasn't. Amanda was now remembering what she had wanted to do to the man when he had invaded her space, but never did because she never wanted to make a scene in front of Adam's friends. While Amanda was envisioning pulling the man's arm off at the shoulder and beating him over the head with it, Adam came up behind her and placed his hand on her hip the same way his friend had done. In the blink of an eye, years of self defense training kicked in and Amanda grabbed the hand at the wrist and in one fluid motion tossed Adam over the rail and into the water.

Amanda heard the surprised yelp from Adam followed by a splash and realised what she had done. She turned to the crew and was surprised to find them laughing and in no hurry to get Adam out of the water. "Aren't you going to help him?"

The female crew member walked to the railing and watched Adam swim to the ladder at the back of the yacht and start to climb out of the water. Once Adam was back on board she turned to Amanda. "Thank you for doing what I have wanted to do for a long time. I dream of doing that each time the owner lets Adam use the yacht."

Amanda was puzzled. "Adam's family doesn't own the yacht?"

"No and they don't own the private jet either. For some unknown reason the boss likes Adam."

Before any more could be said Adam was approaching them and demanding a dry towel which the female crew member handed him. Amanda watched Adam dry himself and admired how the clinging wet shirt enhanced the view of his muscular chest and shoulders.

Adam turned to her as he rubbed his hair with a towel. "It has been quite some time since someone has thrown me."

Amanda instantly started to apologise. "I'm so sorry but you startled me."

Adam started to unbutton his shirt. "I should be the one to say I'm sorry. It won't happen again."Adam pulled his arm from the sleeve and tossed the shirt to one of the crew as he continued to dry himself. Adam slowly reached out his hand and waited until Amanda offered her hand of her own free will. "Breakfast is ready."He then escorted her to the top deck where breakfast was waiting with a breath taking view of the island. Adam motioned towards the island. "I wanted to share the beauty of this island with you while we ate."

Breakfast was divine and Amanda once again found herself imagining what it would be like to enjoy this lifestyle everyday for the rest of her life.

Dale lay in bed and looked at the clock on the end table beside the bed that displayed both the time and date. He took a deep breath and sighed. It was finally his birthday and he couldn't help but think about what his mother always said on birthdays. He imagined being at home and hearing her ask. "Well today you are another year older but are you another year wiser?" Dale rubbed his face with his hands as he tried to think of the answer he might give his mother after the events of this year. He might consider himself to be wiser, but only because he had been foolish.

Dale played with the engagement ring that he felt should be on Amanda's finger if only he hadn't been so foolish and had proposed at any of the times he had felt could be the right time. He looked at the ring through the tears in his eyes as he was once again overcome with the fear that when he saw Amanda again it might be too late for him to propose. He kissed the ring and then held the ring against his chest – next to his heart.

Dale showered and prepared for what had the potential of being the most miserable birthday ever – even worse than the one when he broke his leg jumping his new bicycle off of the roof of the neighbors shed. When he was ready to leave the room Dale stood looking at his reflection in the mirror on the back of the door. For a fleeting moment Dale imagined Amanda was at his side dressed in a white wedding gown with her arms around his and her head resting on his shoulder. The moment ended with the chime of the clock in the town square reminding him of the busy day that lay ahead. He grabbed the breakfast vouchers for the restaurant in the hotel from the corner of the desk; he paused and looked at them for a moment before he set them back on the desk. It was his birthday and he was going to make it the best birthday ever. He was going to stop being concerned over things he had no control over and enjoy the foods that he loved and be with friends as much as possible.

Dale stepped out of the hotel and took a deep breath of the fresh sea air. He watched the sea birds flying in the cloudless sky a few moments before he made his way to breakfast. As he walked along the seaside pathway towards the restaurant there were so many things that reminded him of Amanda that Dale couldn't stop thinking about her. He couldn't stop wondering where she was and if she missed not being here to help him celebrate his birthday as much as he missed not being there for her birthday.

While he stood at the counter waiting to be seated Dale turned to face the town square and watched the people scurrying about in the morning sun. He was lost in his thoughts about the last time he had been here with Amanda and had walked in the square. He began to think about the time that never was and how fortunate they had been to miss the bombing when he was startled by the voice behind him.

"Good morning sir, would you like to sit indoors or outside on the patio?"

Dale recognized the voice and smiled as he turned his back to the town square. "Marcus Sullivan my dear friend it is good to see you again. May I sit at my usual table?"

Marcus took a closer look at his guest before extending his arms. "What a pleasant surprise to see you here." The two men embraced. "I almost didn't recognize you without Amanda at your side." He stepped back and looked around. "Is Amanda going to join you?"

Dale felt a twinge of sadness enter his heart at the mention of Amanda's name. "Not this time. I am in town for the big wedding and Amanda was unable to join me."

Marcus picked up a menu from the counter and motioned for Dale to follow him. They walked past Dale's usual table and moved towards a booth at the back. "I was just going to have breakfast myself and I would be honored to have the pleasure of your company." Marcus signaled to a waiter and ordered for both of them before he sat down across from Dale. "So how are things with you and Amanda? Have you proposed to her yet?"

Dale's shoulders drooped. He took a deep breath and then he sighed as he hung his head. "Marcus I have been a fool."

Marcus waited until the waiter had finished placing their drinks onto the table. "What did you do that was so foolish?"

Dale started to tell the story from the moment he had planned the weeklong vacation with Amanda with the intention of proposing in the town square. It was more difficult for Dale to tell his story than he thought it would be as he remembered all of the opportunities to propose to Amanda he had passed up. Dale swallowed hard and blinked his eyes to clear some tears. "I had planned to propose to Amanda this weekend before being assigned to come to this wedding. Even after being assigned to come here my flight was booked with a layover that would have given me ample time to propose to her."

"So what happened?"

Dale took another deep breath. "When I arrived I found that Amanda had left for the weekend with another man." Dale dabbed his eyes with the napkin."

"Do you know where they went and who the man is?"

Dale sipped his drink. "I have no idea where they went." He took another sip. "The man she is with is a temporary replacement assigned to fill in for me while I was in training for a promotion." Dale placed the glass onto the table with a loud thud and then steadied it so it didn't tip over.

Marcus leaned forward in his chair. "Do you feel that there is a reason to be concerned for Amanda to be with this man?"

Dale sighed. "When I called to speak with Amanda on her birthday; this man answered her phone and never let her know that I had called. Then this man had taunted me by saying he might propose to her that evening, but didn't." Dale took another sip of his drink. "Now here I sit on my birthday not knowing where they are or if it is his intention to propose to her on this weekend excursion."

The waiter placed the plates of food on the table in front of the men.

Dale picked up his fork but only moved the hash brown potatoes around on the plate. "Marcus, what if I blew it and have lost Amanda forever?"

Marcus placed a hand on Dales' arm. "Life is too short to worry about things we have no control over. Amanda is crazy for you and I am certain that you will still have a chance to propose to her." He removed his hand from Dale's arm as he sat back and reached for his utensils. "You may not propose to her on your birthday, but I'm fairly certain that when the next opportunity presents itself – you will seize the moment."

The two men finished their meal and talked until it was time for Dale to leave for the wedding. Before they left the table Marcus placed his hand on Dale's arm. "Dale you need to be back at the restaurant by six o'clock this evening."

"What is going on then?"

Marcus smiled. "My wife and I are going to invite some friends and treat you to an evening of food and entertainment to celebrate your birthday."

Amanda did not believe in coincidence and was bothered to think that Adam's friend Rob and his girlfriend Ginny had just happened to decide on the same destination on the same weekend as her and Adam. Adam claimed to be as surprised as she was and swore that this development wasn't planned and was exactly what he claimed it was –a coincidence. Amanda still did not believe that it was a coincidence and the thought that her weekend might include having to spend time with Rob and Ginny upset her. She hoped that Adam understood how she felt and wouldn't be stupid enough to invite the couple to spend time with them. There was no scenario Amanda could think of where spending another evening in the company of that rude, overbearing, inconsiderate man would end well.

Adam had spent most of the afternoon on the other yacht with Rob and Ginny by himself because Amanda claimed to have had a headache and did not go over with him. Amanda sat on the deck chair and tried to read her book. It was difficult to focus on the book and spent most of her time thinking about Dale being alone on his birthday and wondering what he was doing. The rest of the time had been informative as she spent time talking with the female crew member finding out what she thought about Adam and his friends. It didn't take long to find out that they were not her most favorite human beings when they were using the yacht.

Before the conversation progressed to reveal details it came to an end when Adam returned from the other yacht. Amanda pretended to read her book and ignored Adam as he sat on the other deck chair. When she didn't acknowledge him he cleared his throat and started to speak.

"How is your headache?"

"I'm doing better and by tomorrow morning it should be fine."

Adam sat silent a few moments. "I was hoping that you were feeling well enough to enjoy the evening of dining and dancing ashore that I had planned for tonight."

"Did you invite Rob and Ginny to join us?" Amanda never looked away from the book but the tone in her voice had a distinct edge.

Adam waited for Amanda to look up from the book. "As a matter of fact I did invite them to join us."

Amanda closed her book and looked intently at Adam. "Then you have fun on shore with Rob and Ginny. I look forward to an enjoyable evening on the yacht with my book." She opened the book to the page and found her place.

Adam took the book from her hands and closed it before he placed it on the table beside the deck chair. "I thought that you had fun the last weekend we spent with Rob and Ginny?"

Amanda shifted on her chair. "For the most part the weekend was fun but there were moments I could have done without."

Adam leaned forward and took Amanda by the hand. "So what part of the weekend did you not like?"

Amanda pulled her hand from his and folded her arms across her chest. "I did not like the times that Rob tried to leave a collection of his finger prints all over my body. What I liked even less was hearing you and Ginny making excuses for his bad behavior. The man is a pig."Amanda picked up her book and moved past Adam on her way to her cabin. "Tonight I will not be a part of a foursome if Rob is coming."

CHAPTER TWENTY

Amanda heard the launch from the other yacht roar off into the distance and the sound of the motor had faded by the time Adam knocked on her door.

Adam opened the door when Amanda had given permission and stayed in the door way. "Rob and Ginny have gone ashore to spend the evening by themselves and I was wondering if you would care to join me ashore for the evening?" he smiled his charming smile. "I promise it will be more fun than reading the book. If it will help you make up your mind I can tell you how the book ends."

"You wouldn't dare."

"Maybe I would and maybe I wouldn't. But if we are busy on shore I will have no reason to tell you how it ends."

Amanda was feeling hungry and she was in the mood for a night out on the town. "Rob and Ginny will be doing their own thing without us?" she waited for Adam to respond.

"We will be a couple tonight and not part of a foursome."

Amanda wanted to know how Adam had handled the arrangements. "What did you tell them as the reason that we will not be joining them?"

"I told them that tonight was special and I wanted to share the evening with you and you alone." Adam started to pull the door shut. "I will close the door so that you can change your clothes and join me for a night on the town.

The launch entered the harbour past the tall ships at the entrance. Adam and Amanda were early for their reservations so they walked along the beach and through the town square. They stopped at the bench by the old clock tower and Adam dropped to one knee beside her. Once Adam had his shoelace tied they continued across the town square towards the restaurant. At the restaurant they were escorted to the table that Adam had reserved earlier that day.

Amanda swallowed hard and had to wipe her eyes. This table was the table Dale always reserved and the feelings in her heart told Amanda that she missed Dale.

The waiter pulled back the chair for Amanda to sit on and then pulled the chair for Adam who sat down and then touched Amanda's hand. "How do you like my surprise so far?"

Amanda did not want her feelings for Dale to ruin the evening so she smiled and placed her other hand on his. "It is wonderful."

Adam motioned to the waiter who then left the table.

"That's odd." Amanda said as the waiter walked away.

"What's odd?"

Amanda watched the waiter disappear from view. "The waiter left without asking if we would like something to drink."

"I already pre-ordered the drinks and the meal for the evening so please sit back and enjoy."

Amanda was surprised when the waiter returned with the drinks. Her drink was what she always ordered when she came here with Dale. She wondered how Adam could possibly have known that this was her favorite drink but kept the question to herself.

"So how was your drink?"

Amanda smiled. "It's one of my favorites and done to perfection."

"Excellent." Adam then motioned to the waiter who shortly appeared at the table with the appetisers.

Once again Adam had ordered her favorite item from the appetiser menu. One that she never knew she liked until Dale had insisted that she try it. "I'm impressed that you would have ordered this appetiser. It is quite unusual and not the first choice that would come to mind."

Adam reached out and took her by the hand. "You strike me as an adventurous person so I took a chance when I placed the order." Adam gave her fingers a soft squeeze. "You are pleased with my selection?"

Amanda resisted the urge to pull her hand back and allowed Adam to caress her fingers. "I am very pleased."

"Good." When they were finished the appetisers Adam once again motioned to the waiter.

Soon the waiter was at the table with the entree. When he removed the cover from her dish the aroma from the spices told Amanda that her favorite dish had been ordered without her even seeing it. Amanda looked at Adam."How did you know?"

Adam smiled and winked. "I have a gift for these things." He then turned to the waiter. "Is the special dessert I ordered going to be ready on time?"

"Yes sir, the owner is taking care of it himself."

"Wonderful."

Dale fulfilled his obligation and attended the wedding. The sight of the happy couple brought joy but also brought a pain to his heart. Dale had spent the better part of the day after the ceremony with the groom's sister at his side — and it seemed that she had no intentions of straying very far. She was a lovely young lady and should the situation have been different he would have enjoyed her company even more. As it was he enjoyed her company long enough that he never had time to change his clothes before he arrived at the restaurant for his birthday party.

Dale arrived at the restaurant just after six o'clock and was greeted by his good friend Marcus and his wife, Naomi, before being escorted to a room in the restaurant he had never seen before. Inside the room Dale was surprised to see the effort that had gone into hosting a birthday party for him. There was a quiet elegance to the decor of the room and the table settings. He had only seen such care for detail at official state dinners he had been privileged to attend, and here was this effort put forth for his birthday.

Dale turned to Marcus and Naomi. "I am honored that you would do this for me."

Naomi took Dale by the hand. "It is our pleasure to do this for you."

Marcus took Naomi by her hand and together they lead Dale to a table where a small gift was at one of the place settings. Marcus motioned for Dale to take a seat at the place setting with the gift. Once they were all seated Marcus turned to Dale. "Please open the gift."

Dale opened the gift and examined the contents before he held it in his hand. "Marcus is this gift what I think it is?"

"That all depends on what you think it is."

Dale saw the smile on the faces of his hosts. "Is this the talisman that you have told me so much about? The one that has brought you good luck since it came into your possession?"

Marcus and Naomi both nodded their heads. "Yes, this is the talisman."

"But why would you give it to me?"

Marcus extended his hand and closed Dale's hand around the gift. "This talisman has helped me to attain the desires of my heart. A successful business, the company of good people who I am proud to call my friends, but most of all it has helped me to find happiness in my life in the company of the girl of my dreams." Marcus placed his arm around Naomi. "We wish for you to have this good luck charm in hopes that you may also find happiness with the girl of your dreams." Marcus had a smile that almost hid his face. "But when you see her you need to propose."

Dale rubbed his fingers over the talisman. "Amen to that."

"Good luck finding happiness." Naomi snuggled closer to Marcus who checked his watch when a waiter entered the room and nodded.

"My friend, keep that good luck charm in a safe place and all will be right in your life." Marcus stood and helped Naomi to her feet. "Our guests have arrived and are waiting to meet you."

Dale turned to face the door and saw many people enter the room. Some he knew from previous visits to the island and the others were friends Dale just hadn't met yet. With Marcus and Naomi at his side

Dale greeted each and every guest. He was surprised that one of the guests was the sister of the groom who had been at his side most of the day at the wedding and should still be at the wedding reception.

The party had been more than Dale could have hoped for to celebrate this birthday. Thanks to Marcus and Naomi, Dale had a lot more friends to visit when he returned to the island. The glances from Marcus and Naomi as he visited with the lovely single young ladies told Dale that they were pleased to see that he was enjoying himself.

In spite of how much he was enjoying himself Dale couldn't stop thinking of Amanda. These young ladies were very attractive and seemed very nice but his heart yearned to be with Amanda. Dale was almost relieved to hear Marcus announce that it was almost time to leave for the theater and people should use the washrooms at the restaurant before they left.

Dale walked through the restaurant past his usual table and as he approached the table he noticed the girl with her back to him. He stopped and stepped out of sight as he waited for his pulse to stop racing. Was he mistaken or was Amanda sitting at their usual table. The girl's hair was the same color as Amanda's and the hair style looked familiar. Dale glanced around the corner to get a better look at the man she was with. The man was every bit attractive as the girls at the office had described. His hair was flawless and his clothing fit in all the right places and Dale could feel emotions growing inside that he had only felt for Adam, the mystery man, when he indicated to Dale that he was going to propose to Amanda.

From his vantage point Dale could see the man reach into his pocket and remove a small velvet box. Dale was mortified to think that this man was planning to propose to his Amanda and was ready to burst into the dining room and stop his happiness from being ruined. He had made the first step with clenched fist at the ready when the girl turned her head and Dale could see that she was not his Amanda. Dale took a deep breath and exhaled a cleansing breath. Amanda had a cute nose. Dale continued past the table for a closer look just to be sure as he went to the washroom. Dale gave a sigh of relieve when he knew for sure that the girl being proposed to was not Amanda.

Dale left the washroom and saw the excitement of the girl at the table as she admired the ring on her finger. Dale felt the ring on the chain around his neck and then placed his hand into his pocket and rubbed the talisman.

Dale rejoined Marcus and Naomi at their table. "Thank you so much for the talisman. I can feel the luck it brings already."

"What happened?" Naomi asked.

"While I was walking to the washroom I went past my usual table and from behind the girl looked like Amanda, right down to the way she styles her curly hair and she was with a very attractive man who had a ring in his hand and was preparing to propose."

Marcus winked. "Will I need to do repairs to my restaurant?"

Dale smiled. "Not at all, my friend; I was ready to make a scene until the girl turned her head and I saw her nose."

"What about her nose?" Naomi asked.

Dale chuckled. "The shadow cast by this girl's nose could give a lot more shade on a sunny day than Amanda's nose ever could."

"So there is a happy couple in my restaurant and you are still enjoying your birthday." Marcus signalled to the waiter. "There is a couple at table seven who are very recently engaged. Take them a complimentary bottle of wine and congratulate them on behalf of the owners."

The waiter left the room and Naomi took Marcus by the arm. "You have always been a romantic at heart."

Marcus patted her arm. "Always have been and always will be." Marcus stood and did a quick head count of his quests. "It looks as if we are all here so let us make our way to the theater for the entertainment part of the evening."

CHAPTER TWENTY ONE

dam and Amanda had finished their entrees and they shared a few moments of conversation while the dishes were being cleared from the table.

The waiter approached the table. "And how was everything so far?"

Amanda gave a thumb up. "It has been excellent. Give my compliments to the chef."

The waiter smiled and nodded before he turned to Adam. "And how was your meal sir?"

"It was wonderful."Adam winked at the waiter. "I'm looking forward to dessert."

The waiter topped up the water glasses. "I will be right back with your dessert." The waiter promptly returned to the kitchen.

While the waiter was gone an attractive young lady walked past their table and turned back to look at Adam before she continued on to the washroom. The girls perfume smelled familiar and Amanda recognized it from the letter Adam claimed was from his aunt. A few minutes later the girl returned and stopped beside the table. "Adam what are you doing here?"

Adam started to look uncomfortable. "I am having a meal with my good friend Amanda."

The girl folded her arms and looked at Adam in disgust. "I can see that you are having a meal. What are you doing in town?"

Adam shifted on his chair. "I like the restaurant."

The girl moved close enough that Adam was about to fall off of his chair. "It has only been five months since you and Rob were last here. My mother has a good memory and a real good reason to not like Rob, and since the two of you are friends, she does not like you either." The girl looked around the restaurant. "Is Rob in town with you?"

"Does it look like Rob is here?" Adam motioned towards the other tables.

She looked around the restaurant a second time before returning her gaze to Adam. She then pointed at Adam with purpose. "You should leave the restaurant before my family arrives and find out that you are here." She glanced in the direction of the front door when a group of people arrived and then back to Adam. "Please leave now, I beg of you, No I am warning you. If Rob is in town you and Rob should consider leaving the country now because the two of you are not their most favorite people."

Amanda watched the girl return to the other part of the restaurant before she turned to Adam. "So what was that all about?"

Adam acted as if nothing had happened. "I do not know what she is talking about."

Before Adam could say another word Rob and Ginny came up behind Amanda. "I thought that we would find you here. Adam you are too predictable." Rob clapped his hands together and started to rub them. "Is it time to celebrate?"

"Celebrate what?" Amanda tensed as she glared at Adam. He had assured her that Rob would not be part of the evening yet here was Rob asking if it was time to celebrate something. She was about to speak her mind but remained silent for fear of what she might say.

Rob placed his hands on Amanda's shoulders as he began to rub with his thumbs moving along her spine. "Young lady you are tense. You need to learn how to relax."

The guests from the birthday party had left the restaurant and were making their way along the street to the theater. Dale had a girl on each arm and two others close enough to move in if one of the girls on Dale's arm should lose her grip. As they passed by the front door of a restaurant there was a commotion inside that could be heard from the street. Dale heard a voice with an American accent speaking in a threatening manner and for a brief moment thought that he might get involved.

Marcus looked back at Dale who was staring at the restaurant door. "What are you going to do my friend?"

Dale shook his head. "I should stop some fellow countrymen from doing something stupid that might land them in jail." He looked at the girls on each arm and decided not to allow the misfortunes of others ruin the rest of his birthday. He smiled at Marcus. "We are going to the theater."

Naomi stood beside Marcus as he held the large theater door open for his friends. "Please find your seats as the production is about to begin."

As Dale passed by Naomi he found it hard to miss the look in her eyes. It was the same look he saw in his sister's eyes when she felt that she had found a girl for Dale. He smiled politely and as he walked past Naomi he winked while he mouthed the words "Thank you."

Naomi snuggled closer to Marcus and mouthed the words. "You're welcome."

Dale took his seat and waited until the young ladies had settled into their seats before he got comfortable. He considered that he was fortunate that he never had to scratch an itch on his nose during the performance because the young ladies holding his arms in theirs made it difficult to move. When he returned to his seat after the intermission Dale found that the seating arrangement had changed and different young ladies would now be holding onto his arms for the second half of the show. Dale glanced over at Marcus and Naomi who had big smiles on their faces as they watched Dale and could only wonder what they had said to the young ladies when they were invited to the party.

After the show most of the party guests said their goodbyes and left. Soon the only people left in the theater lobby with Dale were Marcus,

Naomi, and the young ladies who seemed to be waiting for Dale to decide who he was going to escort home.

Marcus had already planned ahead and had taxi vouchers for the young ladies. Soon Dale was the last man standing with Marcus and Naomi at the theater. Dale thanked them for showing him such a wonderful time for his birthday.

Marcus had a large grin on his face as he took Dale by the hand. "That Talisman seems to be working for you already with the ladies."

Dale reached into his pocket and removed the coin. "This much good luck could be a dangerous thing."

Naomi took Dale by the hand. "If you would like the numbers of any of the girls at the party I will get them for you." She winked. "I think Carla really likes you."

"What makes you say that?"

Naomi smiled. "She must like you enough to leave a family wedding party."

Dale pulled a hand full of papers from his pocket. "I think that they all like me. Each of them slipped a piece of paper with their name and number into my pocket."

CHAPTER TWENTY TWO

Amanda had caught a glimpse of the engagement ring on the dessert tray before it fell to the floor with the desserts. Amanda stood in front of the mirror in the washroom looking at her reflection as she cleaned the dessert splatter from the front of her clothes. As she stood there she couldn't help but wonder what had caused her to toss Rob with such enthusiasm that she broke a chair and knocked the waiter to the ground; instead of using just enough force to send a message to him to stop touching her. Had her reaction been a result of her growing disgust for the man from previous encounters? Or had something else caused her to do what she did?

Amanda checked to make sure that she hadn't missed any spots and was about to return to the table when she stopped and thought about some more questions about her behavior. Had she reacted the way that she did as a means to disrupt the evening and avoid hearing a marriage proposal from Adam she wasn't ready to hear? Amanda thought about the question and shook her head. Until that girl had stopped to talk and Adam had become so uncomfortable; Amanda would have considered a proposal and might even have said yes. Now she wasn't so sure. Did she know Adam well enough to make a decision that would affect the rest of her life?

Amanda returned to the table and waited for Adam. She suspected that he was still in the washroom. Rob and Ginny were nowhere to be found; a development which didn't upset her in the least. She was glad that he was smart enough to leave before she became really upset. Enough time had passed that Amanda was becoming concerned about what was taking Adam so long.

The waiter approached the table with a small plate and placed it on the table next to her. On the plate was a slip of paper she assumed was the bill for the meal, two mints, and a velvet ring box. "Why are you giving this to me?" Amanda picked up the box and opened it. The ring inside was exquisite, even with the piece of fruit stuck to the corner of the large diamond.

As Amanda admired the ring the waiter spoke. "We would have returned the ring to the gentleman but he had already left the restaurant with his friends." He motioned towards the plate. "They left without paying the bill."

Amanda looked at the paper and cringed before she even looked at the side with the writing on it. After she saw the total she began to feel ill; the price of the wine and the champagne was more than the remaining limit on her credit card; then there was the price for the meal and the dessert that no one had tasted.

Dale left the theater and considered calling it a night. He was about to walk across the street to his hotel when his curiosity about the commotion at the restaurant earlier got the better of him. When he arrived at the restaurant he couldn't help but notice the dessert stain on the waiter's pant leg. He approached the waiter.

"Earlier this evening I heard a commotion inside the restaurant as I was walking past with friends. Can you tell me what happened?"

The waiter looked at Dale. "Which time?"

"There was more than one?"

The waiter placed some menus behind the counter. "Yes, but I think the incidents were related."

Dale was intrigued. "What was the first incident?"

The waiter handed Dale a dessert menu and motioned towards a table.

Dale took a seat and ordered some ice cream. "So what happened?"

The waiter smiled. "This man was planning to propose to his girl during dessert. The ring was to be delivered with the dessert and that is the time that the girl lost it."

Dale thought about what the waiter had said and wanted to clarify the response. "You're telling me that the girl lost it when she saw the ring?"

"No she lost it when the man's friend came up behind her and placed his hands on her shoulders." The waiter smiled. "She tossed the man like a rag doll, breaking one of the dining room chairs with him as he went to the floor."

Dale smiled as he played with the visual in his mind. "Then what happened?"

The waiter raised his pant leg to show a red patch of skin that looked like it was going to bruise. "The man's leg hit me on his way to the floor and caused me to lose control of the dessert tray, dropping the desserts onto the people and the floor."

Dale chuckled. "So what was the second commotion?"

The waiter brought Dale the ice cream and a glass of water. "It would seem that some other diners do not like the two men. When the first commotion occurred the two men were recognized and they were chased from the restaurant and down the street with one of the girls."

Dale was curious. "What happened to the other girl?"

"She was in the washroom when the men fled to escape the pursuit."

"Do you know where the girl is now?"

The waiter brought Dale his bill. "She left after settling the bill for the meal – and she was a generous tipper."

Dale caught the hint and left a generous tip. "Is there anything else you can tell me?"

The waiter collected the money from the table. "That is all that I can tell you."

Amanda strolled down the beach and enjoyed the calming sound of the tide lapping on the sand. She was still annoyed that Adam had left the restaurant while she was in the washroom; leaving her to pay the bill. Amanda stopped walking when she heard voices behind her and turned to watch a young couple walking arm in arm with the girl resting her head on the man's shoulder. Amanda looked at her empty ring finger and smiled. This weekend with Adam and his friends had reinforced to her that she loved Dale and would be miserable without him. She wanted to be with him and was willing to wait for a proposal that my never come. She scolded herself for even considering a life with that scoundrel Adam and shuddered to think that she might have considered a marriage proposal for some very superficial reasons.

Amanda smiled as she thought about how colleagues had called Dale the playboy diplomat. Were they ever wrong; Dale was a boy scout compared to Adam. She thought about the private jet and the yacht Adam had claimed belonged to his family, but according to the crew was just made available to Adam. She thought about the gorgeous engagement ring with the exquisite diamond the waiter had returned to her with the bill. The ring should have been worth more than enough to cover the bill for the meal and the damages – unless it was a fake like Adam. If it was then the waiter would be stuck with a very nice cubic zirconium ring and the bill.

Amanda kicked at the waves as she walked along the sand and enjoyed the solitude. Once back in town she stopped in the town square and sat on the bench beside the majestic clock tower. She saw a falling star and made a wish. "Dale I wish that I could have been with you on your birthday."

The clock started to chime and announce the midnight hour. Amanda heard a noise behind her and turned to look over her left shoulder. Her initial glance behind her had revealed that she was alone. Before she could turn to look over her right shoulder Amanda heard a voice that made her gasp. She quickly turned to her right and saw Dale at her side on one knee with a ring in his hand, saying the words she had been longing to hear him say. "Amanda Pike will you marry me?"